Frank glanced s[...]ed anxiously and ask[...]ell with the other plot [...]

"Well enough," said Mrs. Ferry.

"With those who wish to get on well with us," said Mr. Ferry. "We don't mix intimately with them—" *For obvious reasons which don't need spelling out,* thought Don "—but we find them agreeable enough."

"They call us The Family, you know." Mrs. Ferry's words seemed to cause an intensification of the universal beam.

Frank knew what was coming next—he knew Weed's list off by heart now—but he was too slow to prevent it. As he opened his mouth to ask a question, any question, he heard Don say, "Actually, Mrs. Ferry, they call you the Addams Family. There's a subtle difference."

The beam flickered, but did not falter. However, all eight Addams Family eyes turned their gaze upon Frank, and did not stray from him for the remainder of the interview. Don Packham no longer existed in the sight of The Family. He had been excommunicated.

★

UP
AND
DOWN

Mat Coward

W🌐RLDWIDE®

TORONTO • NEW YORK • LONDON
AMSTERDAM • PARIS • SYDNEY • HAMBURG
STOCKHOLM • ATHENS • TOKYO • MILAN
MADRID • WARSAW • BUDAPEST • AUCKLAND

To all allotment gardeners, everywhere.
The land is ours!

UP AND DOWN

A Worldwide Mystery/February 2004

First published by Five Star.

ISBN 0-373-26484-4

Copyright © 2000 by Mat Coward.

Printed in U.S.A.

Author's Note

Under British law, councils in cities, towns, suburbs and villages are required to provide pieces of land for rent, for local residents to use as gardens. These gardens are known as allotments. They are valued by people who live in flats with no gardens of their own, and by enthusiastic hobby gardeners. Generally speaking, they are cheerful, friendly places—and much less deadly than the entirely fictional allotment site depicted in this book.

ONE

THE CRIME SCENE at Crockett's Drive allotment site was easily identifiable, even from the road.

"That'll be us," said PC Standfield, pointing towards the far end of the site, where a dozen or so people, allotmenteers presumably, could be seen huddling on the path which ran between the two rows of plots.

"I imagine so," said Frank Mitchell, his mildly Geordie tones hiding from untutored southern ears any suggestion of sarcasm.

The two PCs got out of their patrol car, and made their way towards the watching knot of gardeners. Their pace was steady, not hurried, their expressions blank, in readiness.

"We got a reporter's name?" asked Standfield.

"No," Frank replied. "Pay phone. But it'll be one of this lot here."

Both officers were feeling watchful, rather than nervous. A report of a body found could mean just about anything, from a shop window dummy floating in a pond, to the start of a serial killer hunt; from an irritating waste of time, to a life-long nightmare. Could be anything.

As they drew closer to the reception committee, a red-faced, barrel-chested man of nearer sixty than fifty broke away from the pack, and puffed his way down the path to meet them. "You'll want CID," were his first words. "Scenes of Crime Officers, forensics, one of those big tents. You'll want the lot here, officer. The *lot.*"

He spoke to Frank Mitchell, not to Les Standfield, nor to both of them, as if instinctively identifying the natural leader. This gave Frank a quick stab of deep pleasure. He longed to replace the *Police Constable* before his name with *Detective* Constable; indeed, at twenty-five, he had already been in uniform a lot longer than he'd hoped or expected to be when he joined the force.

"I'm afraid you'll have to make do with us for now, sir. If you'd like to show us what you've found…?"

"Ah, yes," said the spokesman (self-appointed, would be Frank's guess). "Triage—quite so, makes sense. Well, I don't think you'll be disappointed. If you'd like to follow me."

"Thank you, Mr.—?"

"Gorringe, Constable. Rodney Gorringe."

"Thank you, Mr. Gorringe." Frank turned to his partner. "Les, do you want to get the other names?"

Les didn't, judging by his face. What he wanted to do was have a good peer at the alleged corpse, just in case it did turn out to be a famous murder victim— the victim, that is, of a soon-to-be famous murderer. Not much point telling the tale, in years to come, of how you were first on the scene, if you had to end it with *Mind you, I never actually saw the stiff—I was too busy with me notebook at the time.*

On the other hand, he couldn't exactly refuse, could he? Bloody Frank Mitchell with his bloody A Levels.

Stuck-up Northern tosser. Hasn't been stationed here ten minutes and he's giving bloody orders. *I hope he does make CID*, thought Les. He'll be right at home with that lot.

While Les took names, Frank followed Mr. Gorringe along the path, and behind a large, slightly tumble-down shed, onto one of the allotments. "Right, Mr. Gorringe," he said, putting his hand lightly on the man's forearm, to prevent him going any further. Just in case this really was something; you never knew. "It's best if you just point it out to me now, and I'll make my own way."

Gorringe nodded towards the other side of the eighty-by-thirty foot plot (ten poles by three, Frank remembered, from his own granddad's allotment, back home). "In the trench," said Gorringe. "His name's Beans."

Frank thought he must have misheard that last bit, but never mind—plenty of time for identification later. Let's rule out the shop window dummy factor, first of all.

Out-ruling was, in the event, a fairly simple matter. *"Bugger my cat,"* muttered Frank, as he caught his first sight of the dead man in the bean trench. The deceased had a garden fork through his throat, and wore a proportionately unhappy expression. He was an old man, insubstantial looking.

Frank didn't feel like throwing up, for which he was grateful. He'd done a course, at his last posting, so he didn't feel totally hopeless. In fact, as long as he was still wearing that uniform, his duties under such circumstances were fairly simple and easy to remember: preserve the scene, and send for the detectives.

He picked his way carefully back across the allotment, retracing his footsteps to the path as precisely as possible. "Les!" he called. "Over here a minute, if you would."

Quick to take offence, but equally quick to get bored with sulking, Les Standfield gave his colleague a friendly, inquiring smile as he trotted over to join him. "What we got?" he asked. "A result? Anything tasty?"

"Oh, Christ yes," said Frank. "We've got a real one here, mate. Better give CID a shout, pronto." Dead gardeners were definitely a job for the Criminal Investigation Department.

"Told you," said Rodney Gorringe, eavesdropping unashamedly and beaming smugly.

IT WAS A Sunday morning in late April: warm and sunny, perfect gardening weather at a perfect gardening time, in a north London suburb which was wealthy enough to support a high level of industrious leisure, but not so grand as to render such muddy pastimes socially impossible. Crockett's Drive allotment site was enjoying a good turnout.

Before long another name was added to its attendance register—that of Detective Inspector Don Packham of Cowden CID.

Frank Mitchell watched his approach with some interest. On seeing the inspector get out of his car, parked next to the patrol car, Les Standfield had said, "Oh shit, not him! I'm off," and gone to take everybody's names and addresses for a second time.

Mr. Packham's reputation certainly preceded him, and was certainly unflattering, but in a rather vague way. All Frank knew for sure, after six weeks at his new nick, was that, "You don't want to have anything to do with DI Packham. Steer clear, mate."

And yet, here was the bogeyman himself, catching a case as was his right on Sunday duty, walking briskly up the main site path towards Frank and his crime scene. And what Frank saw was a conventionally (and cleanly) dressed man of about 40; just under six feet tall, of wiry build—more of a runner than a rugby player. His hair was short but thick, although forming a clear widow's peak at the front, and very black. He seemed good-looking enough; though with, perhaps, a set of features too well-defined for modern tastes.

Most surprising of all, DI Packham's face wore a cheerful smile, and his arm was raised, acknowledging Frank with a friendly, informal wave.

"You Frank Mitchell?" The formerly waving hand was held out for shaking as DI Packham drew level with the short, red-headed young plod.

"Yes, sir." Frank took the firm handshake, and returned it gently, with due deference for rank.

"I'm DI Packham. Don."

"Yes, sir."

Don looked around the site, smiling and sniffing the air. "Good to get out in the country for a day, eh?"

Frank assumed this was a joke—Crockett's Drive was a pleasant enough spot, but unmistakably suburban—and warily responded in kind. "Yes, sir. A rare treat for the lungs, sir."

"You a Geordie?" asked Don.

"That's right, sir."

"Excellent!" said Don, enthusiastically. "I used to

have a girlfriend from Newcastle. But don't worry—she didn't have red hair.''

Frank laughed, though he wasn't entirely sure what at.

"And your big mate over there—the one who looks like a grandson of Leighton Rees. Who's he?''

"That's Les Standfield, sir,'' said Frank, not even bothering to wonder who Leighton Rees was. Some 60s rock idol, presumably.

"Fine,'' said Don. "So, let's see what we've got. And it's Don, remember, when there's no audience, not Sir.''

"Right you are,'' said Frank, neatly sidestepping that particular minefield of etiquette.

Looking down into the bean trench, Frank couldn't help but notice that the man with the fork in his throat was still there. Don Packham knelt at the edge of the trench and hummed under his breath as he took in the scene.

"Won't have to spend long looking for the weapon, then,'' he said, standing up again.

"I suppose not,'' said Frank. "Unless…well, no, obviously.''

Don nodded. "No, no, you're quite right, Frank. Don't take anything for granted. He could have been dead when the fork went in. Although, judging from the amount of blood in the vicinity of the wound that seems unlikely. Got a name for him?''

"Les is on to that now,'' said Frank. "He's corralled the witnesses over by the main path, as you see.''

"Right,'' said Don. "We'll go and have a word in a moment. Let's get our feet off the plot, so we don't give Scenes of Crime anything to moan about." They tiptoed back to the edge of the allotment. "Looks suspiciously like a shallow grave, doesn't it? Where he's lying?"

"It's a bean trench, sir. Don. It's, like, a trench for…" Frank trailed off, hoping it didn't sound as if he'd just knighted the DI.

"For beans? I see. Don't they grow up poles?"

"They do, yes, but you see, over the winter, up until springtime, some gardeners like to dig out a trench and gradually fill it with kitchen waste, stuff from the garden and so on. It gives the beans a good root run—lots of food and moisture. I imagine he'd have been about due to fill it in now, ready for sowing the beans, or maybe planting them out, in a few weeks' time. It was his allotment, by the way, according to one of the other plotholders. The dead man's."

"Very good," said Don. "Very useful bit of insight, Frank. Well done. You a gardener, then?"

"Not really, sir. My granddad was—had an allotment not unlike this one. On a railway line, too."

"Well, I can see that's going to be very handy, having a horticultural expert on hand."

Frank's heart blinked: did that mean what it sounded like it meant? Was he going to be on the investigation? Christ, that'd be a result! Ah, but no, surely that wasn't how they did things in CID.

"Are we expecting AMIP, sir?" he asked.

Don laughed, and lit a small cigar from a tin case. He offered one to Frank, who shook his head; he sometimes smoked a pipe at home, but knew he was too youthful to get away with it in public. "I have informed Area," Don confirmed. "And I daresay Detective Superintendent Potter will be along imminently. But to tell you the truth, I'm not sure she'll be in a great hurry to take it away from us.''

"No?" said Frank, thinking: *Us—he said us!*

''We'll see,'' Don said, with a wink. He turned slowly on his heels, smoke drifting from between his teeth, as he took in the entirety of the locus.

Frank did likewise, minus the smoke, and saw a standard-enough allotment site, consisting of about twenty individual allotments, most the same size as that which contained the corpse. The site was approximately oblong, at least twice as long as it was wide, bordered at the top by a quiet, residential road, at the bottom by a railway line (or more precisely an overground Tube line), and on each side by the gardens of private houses, their bournes well defended by thick hedges of conifer and holly.

"Tell you what," said Don. "There's only one practical means of access here, isn't there? Through the gate at the top. I mean, I can't see anyone but a Jack Russell terrier getting through from any of those gardens, can you? And that fence along the Metropolitan Line looks serious enough to guard a missile base. Agreed?''

It took Frank a moment to realise that the DI was genuinely seeking his opinion. He'd been in the force ever since he left the sixth form with A Levels in Business Studies, Management and German, but he couldn't remember a senior officer ever wanting his opinion before. Was that why people told him to keep clear of Packham?

"Agreed," he said. "Agreed, Don, absolutely.''

"So assuming that the old gent was killed where he

now sleeps—which of course we are *not* assuming," he added, with a slight bow towards Frank, "then the killer came through that gate there, up the main dividing path, and down that secondary path to reach the scene of death. Yes? The exact same route I've just taken, in fact."

"I would certainly say so," said Frank. And then, because he had never been afraid to speak his mind to anyone, provided he was sure he knew what he was talking about, he added, "Something else struck me."

Don nodded, smiled. "Yes? Great, let's hear it."

"Well, sir, it occurs to me that you can't actually see the bean trench from anywhere else on the site. You see, where it's positioned—top left corner of the top left plot—it's obscured by the hedge of one of the private gardens, the railway line, that plot's shed and a shed on one of the other plots."

"Hmm," said Don, smoking his cigar and stroking his cheek.

"So you see, sir, it would be a pretty private place for a killing."

"Hmm," said Don again. "I was just wondering—do you suppose he got enough light there? For runner beans?" Frank spent five or six seconds trying to think of a sufficiently detective-like response, but was saved from delivering one by Don's, "Yes, you're absolutely right, Frank. Good thinking, you're absolutely right."

Frank thought he could sniff a hint of the country in the DI's voice; not quite an accent, exactly, but a slight suggestion of a burr, like the noise a cat makes when it's too near sleep to purr out loud. West Country, was it?

"So," said Don, "you don't know his name but

you do know it was his allotment? Fine, not to worry, we'll have a word with your pal. Les, is it?''

''That's right. Les.'' Frank hoped that this was not going to be an embarrassing encounter, given his fellow constable's earlier reactions to the mere sight of Don Packham's motor.

However, as they approached Les Standfield and his herd of witnesses, Les called over to them, ''Sir! Funfair's in town!'' and pointed towards the road, which several more vehicles were now clogging up.

''Right,'' said Don. ''Frank—you do the business here, OK? I'll go and suck up to management.''

MANAGEMENT, IN THIS instance, was Detective Superintendent Rosemary Potter of the Area Major Investigations Pool, who Don had known for years as a powerful, intelligent, completely cynical empire-builder. She looked like a shot-putter and dressed like a TV executive. She was quite fond of DI Packham, because he was so very obviously not a man who would ever make DCI.

''Don, love, great to see you!'' They pumped hands. ''We must stop meeting like this.'' Don firmly believed that ''Pansy'' Potter had a list of ice-breaking clichés which she used in strict rotation, regardless of relevance or context. Occasionally, by pure chance, the gag more or less fitted the situation. ''So what have you got for me?''

For a moment Don was tempted to reply *A stiff, ma'am* but was afraid that she might take it the right way. It would be disastrous to let Pansy Potter think you were sexually harassing her; suicidal to let her think you wanted to be sexually harassed by her.

"Not much, Boss," he said, instead, with a dismissive frown. "Some old geezer, cloth cap and suit trousers. Pronged to death amid his turnips. Looks like manslaughter from here. Definitely not page-one material."

Superintendent Potter rocked back on her heels, the better to smile into Don's eyes. "You know me too well, don't you, Donny-boy? Or you bloody think you do." Her voice was raspy—not from too many cigarettes, Don suspected, but from untrained attempts to sound husky in front of press conference microphones.

"Not too well, Pansy, no." He spread his hands in a gesture of innocence. "Just well enough to save you wasting your time. The present deceased is male, elderly, probably working-class, and grows vegetables for pleasure. This case simply has not got 'Potter of the Yard' written all over it."

Potter was quiet for a moment. She walked small circles on her short legs and big feet, with her plump hands in her expensive pockets, her large square head staring at the ground.

"OK," she said at last. "You're one of the few men in this force I would actually trust on something like this, Don. And I don't mean that as a compliment."

"Thank you, ma'am," said Don.

"So you can have it. God knows I've got enough to be going on with." Her eyes sparkled suddenly, making her almost attractive. "We've got a brilliant one over in Harrow—have you heard?"

Don nodded, and at the same time signalled behind Potter's back to the various Scene of Crime Officers and other specialists who had been waiting for permission to move on to the plot. "The young girl? Yeah, I heard about it. Is it really Satanism?"

"I bloody hope so!" she replied, bobbing her head towards him and pulling a face like a child anticipating Christmas. "Anyway, details. What sort of team do you want?"

Don shook his head. "You know me, Boss. I'm a cheap date. I'll just second one of the local uniforms, if you could arrange that for me." They both knew that such a request coming from Don himself would not be sympathetically met. "A lad called Frank Mitchell would do nicely. He's a PC."

"Why him in particular?"

"He was first on the scene. Anyway, turns out he knows everything about allotment gardening."

"Jesus!" said Potter. "How old is he?"

Don shrugged. "Early twenties? Twenty-five?"

"Jesus!" she said again. "What a sad case! Remind me never to give him a job in CID."

TWO

FRANK WATCHED the conversation between the two senior officers with some interest. He was too far away, of course, to hear what they had to say to each other, but there certainly seemed to be plenty of it, accompanied by smiles and laughter and mock-angry finger-wagging. Perhaps they were…God, no—surely not! If they were, Don'd be at least a DCI by now.

Meanwhile, Frank copied all the details of the witnesses from Les's book into his own—not a waste of time, not if it kept Les and Don apart—and showed the forensics people, and the rest of the travelling circus, where they could find the late Mr. Arthur Jones.

By the time Don Packham returned from his conference with the Detective Superintendent, Frank had even got an address for the deceased, from the town hall allotment department, via the Cowden nick radio control room.

The address was only five minutes walk from the allotments. So, leaving the specialists to do their work, and Les Standfield to watch them doing it, Don and Frank took a walk round there. On the way, Frank read from his notebook. Now officially seconded to the investigation, he was determined to impress.

"People called him 'Beans,'" he said. "Most of them didn't know his real name, said he'd been introduced to them, or more likely just pointed out to them, as Beans, and that was how they thought of him."

"Beans because he was full of them?" asked Don.

"In a way, yes. Seems he grew almost nothing but beans. Runner beans, broad beans, French beans. Obviously didn't go in much for crop rotation."

"For what rotation?" said Don, sounding genuinely curious.

Frank wished he hadn't spoken. "Um, not sure entirely, sir. Something I remember the old boys talking about on my granddad's plot. To do with putting the different vegetables in different places so they don't...so they wouldn't..."

"Miscegenate?" Don suggested.

"Possibly, sir. Anyway, he grew a lot of beans, and it obviously suited him because he's been doing it for at least twenty-three years."

"Twenty-three?" said Don. "That seems a very precise number to have 'at least' put in front of it?"

"That's how far back the local authority's allotment records go, sir. Don. But according to a couple of the other plotters—"

"Plotters! Nice one!" Don laughed.

"Sir. According to a couple of them, Beans had been there more or less since the dawn of time."

"Which is longer than twenty-three years, is it?"

"Since the 1950s, was one guess."

"Good God," said Don. "All those beans! Socrates would have been horrified."

"Socrates the philosopher?" asked Frank, a bit lost.

Don tapped his head, screwed up his eyes. "My memory's excellent, Frank, but my powers of recall aren't what they might be. I *think* it was Socrates who was anti-beans. But it could have been Oliver Cromwell. Or Pele, even. I don't know, just something I read.''

''Ah,'' said Frank. That explained it. He should have known the DI was a reader: he had that kind of distracted excitement about him that Frank had so often observed in readers. Frank himself was no reader. That is, he always had a book ''on the go,'' always one he'd heard about on BBC2 or Radio 4 or from one of the broadsheet dailies, always read it dutifully before going to sleep, and never enjoyed it. Enjoying it wasn't the point: you read because it was what people of a certain level in society did. His wife was an indiscriminately enthusiastic reader of magazines, which didn't count, Frank reckoned. Still, it gave her great pleasure, and he often bought her a magazine she hadn't tried before on his way home. Didn't matter what the subject was—motorbikes, golf, paranormal phenomena—she loved them all.

Don Packham, on the other hand—and yes, now Frank came to look, all the signs were there; the jokes, the small cigars, the face-pulling—Don was clearly someone who read for pleasure. Like the difference between a recreational drug user and someone who takes paracetamol for flu. And look where it had got him: couldn't tell the difference between Socrates and Pele.

''You've let the other plotters go, have you?'' Don asked.

''Yes, sir,'' said Frank. ''Apart from the bloke who actually discovered the body. I asked Les to keep him for a while, in case you wanted to have a word later.''

''Good. With a bit of luck he'll be the perpetrator.''

Arthur Jones had lived in a council-owned maisonette in what Don said was a "semi-sheltered" cul-de-sac; that is, it wasn't sheltered housing in the sense of having wardens and common rooms, but it wasn't quite the outside world either, in that nobody under the age of sixty lived there.

"Here we are, sir—number three."

"And we don't know for sure if he lived alone or not?"

"No, sir. Nobody else on the electoral register, though."

"All right. Listen, Frank, sorry about this, but if there's news to be broken, you'll have to do the breaking. You're the one wearing a uniform."

This had occurred to Frank. "Yes, sir." All those beans, he thought: he could never have got through all those on his own. Probably got a wife, six kids and a hundred grandchildren.

"But first, we'll ask around. He's the upstairs flat? Right, let's give downstairs a knock."

In the event, it took fifteen minutes and seven knocks before they found a resident who was at home, and who had ever spoken so much as a word to the old gent in number three. North London suburbs were not, as a rule, gregarious environments.

But Miss Leicher at number eight was in, was willing to talk to the police, and counted Arthur Jones as: "Well, not exactly a friend, I wouldn't say, because they don't really go in for that round here. I'm from the East End myself, you can probably tell, came out here in the 1930s for the fresh air if you can believe that. Ha! Fresh air! Still, you don't want to hear all that. The point is, Cowden people don't have friends, they got video recorders instead, and caravans some of them, but Arthur was, shall we say, a friendly neighbour. He fed my cat when I was in hospital, and we had each other's door keys, and we both enjoyed chatting about the old days. And I'm very sorry he's dead. Very sorry. But he's only himself to blame, messing about on that allotment at his age. I could have predicted he'd have an accident down there sooner or later. In fact, I did predict it, several times. Though I never hoped it would come true. Would you like some brandy in that tea? I'm going to. I could bloody do with one, I can tell you, pardon my German.''

Brandies were declined, at some length, and eventually Frank got a chance to ask: ''Did you say you had a key to his flat, Miss Leicher?''

''Certainly I have, young man. But you've got his, haven't you? He must have had it on him, he carried it on a chain.''

''No,'' Frank began, ''it's still, well, it's still…''

''Still on him?'' said Miss Leicher. ''Well, he won't be wanting it, will he? You could have taken that without anyone calling you a thief, I should have thought.''

''No, the thing is,'' Frank explained, ''we're not allowed to interfere with the, with the deceased person's, his person, until he's been—until the undertaker has seen him.'' Out in the street, Don had said *Accident, all right? Don't mention murder or we'll be here all day.*

''Is that right? Well, I suppose it's only respectful, though I've never been one for religion myself. I mean, if there's a god, where did I get this from?''

Miss Leicher banged her arthritic hip with a walking stick.

Probably from banging it with that stick, thought Frank. But he smiled, nodded, and left the rest of the interview to Don.

Skilful and patient questioning elicited the information that Beans had been seventy-eight years old, a retired printer, a long-time widower, had lived alone, and had no surviving family, with the possible exception of a distant cousin in America, Canada or Australia. But definitely not New Zealand.

And finally, they got the key.

ARTHUR "BEANS" JONES'S one-bedroom maisonette was clean but dingy, furnished not only in the styles of forty years ago, but, to a large extent, with items actually acquired forty years ago.

Not that there was much of anything. In the hall, a telephone table. In the bedroom a bed, chest, wardrobe and straight-backed chair. In the living room, a sofa, armchair, two dining chairs, small coffee table, TV, one bookcase. No dining table.

"This was a man who lived in the past," said Don, and Frank wondered whether this was meant to be some sort of pun. Or did the inspector fancy himself a psychic? Certainly, from the way he'd tiptoed into the flat, nose extended at full sniff, eyes half-closed, fingertips ostentatiously tingling, mystic powers did not seem entirely out of the question.

"Wherever he lived," said Frank, "he didn't live much. Did he? Looking round here, I mean."

"Ah, but Frank, he had his passion, didn't he?"

"Passion?" Frank had just been thinking how mercilessly womanless this flat felt.

Don Packham lit one of his mini cigars and sat down on Beans's sofa. "What's your passion, Frank? Tells you everything you need to know about a person, I always think, if you find out what their passion is. So how about you?"

Frank racked his mind for an acceptable answer. Cooking? Well, Debbie had bought him that pasta maker for Christmas, and he did find that a therapeutic and satisfying activity. And he enjoyed watching Debbie eat the pasta after he made it, with appreciative noises. Himself, he could take fresh pasta or leave it alone: same went for all food, really, he didn't understand the fuss. Just fuel, that's all it was. But, yes, he did enjoy cooking for his wife.

Other than that...well, he quite liked watching sport on TV. Any sport, didn't matter which, sat there on the big settee with Debbie on a Saturday afternoon, lulled half to sleep by the soporific hysteria of the commentators.

He could say either of those, he supposed, give those as his passion. He certainly wasn't going to tell the truth, wasn't going to say: my wife. But he hesitated to lie, feeling instinctively that whatever he said now he'd be stuck with for as long as he and DI Packham worked for the same force. Ten years from now, Don could be ringing him up for advice on how to get his sponges to rise.

And then, *ah!* Inspiration. With a chuckle, and a slight broadening of the Geordie accent, he said, "I can see why you're the DI and I'm the PC."

Don's smile deepened. "Yes?"

"Well, you're pretty bloody good at getting info out of people aren't you? You know all about me, where I come from, me granddad's allotment, what have you. But I know nothing about you."

Don laughed, waved his cigar expansively—a touching gesture, when it involved such a very small cigar. "Ask away, Frank!"

"No, I won't ask—I'll tell. Show you what a good detective I am. For instance, your passion: books, am I right? You're a big reader."

Don looked up at the yellow-stained ceiling and blew some more smoke at it. "Well," he said, "you're right, and then again—you're right. That is to say, Frank, reading is indeed one of the roof beams of my life. But it's so central to my existence—such an enduring, invariably reliable source of solace and joy—that I don't even count it as a passion. You see, I asked you the wrong question. I said passion. It should have been passions. Plural. For instance, did I ever tell you I used to play darts at county level?"

Having absolutely no idea whether or not this was a rhetorical question, Frank decided to move on. Or back, rather, to the matter in hand. "So, apart from growing beans, what were Beans's passions?"

Don gestured towards the bookcase. "Local history, judging by the titles there, and from what Miss Leicher said. But," he added, looking around him again, "not much else. You're right, Frank: no one's done much living here, not since Mrs. Beans died, at least."

BACK AT THE DEATH SCENE, Don and Frank found many of their scientific colleagues had been and gone. Arthur Jones, however, was still amongst those present.

"Problem is, Inspector," a tubby, bald crime scene man explained, with some relish, "if we tried to lift him out of the trench with the fork still in place, there was a risk of it toppling over and disfiguring the wound. While on the other hand, what with the narrowness and depth of the trench, it was very difficult to remove the fork without trampling all over the scene. So what we did in the end was—"

"Excellent," Don interrupted. "Well done. Good work, all."

He found the pathologist admiring a stand of purple sprouting broccoli on an adjoining allotment. "Afternoon, Mr. Walker. You another secret gardener, are you?"

Sam Walker, a thin, bearded man in his late fifties, looked up as Don approached. "Hello, Inspector. Secret gardener? Well, no secret about it. My wife and I haven't eaten a shop-bought vegetable since we moved to our present place five years ago. Mind you, wish I could get my purple sprouting as stocky as this chap gets his. Lighter soil where we are, you see: root-rock. It's a bastard for brassicas."

"Right," said Don, thinking that maybe next time he moved he'd try and get himself a decent patch of garden. They all looked well enough on it, these gardeners, that was for sure. Except old Beans, obviously.

"So," said Walker, turning his attention reluctantly from the broccoli. "You'll want my preliminaries, yes?"

"If you would, Mr. Walker. And thanks for waiting for me."

Walker laughed. "I wasn't—I was just lost in admiration of all this lot."

"You're a lucky man," said Don, "whose job allows him such opportunities to pursue his hobbies."

The pathologist gave him a theatrically stern look over the top of gold-rimmed spectacles. "Never call it a hobby, Inspector. Gardening is definitely not a hobby."

"Oh, right. A way of life, I suppose?"

"Nor even that," said Walker. "Gardening is life."

"I'll keep it in mind," Don promised solemnly.

"All right, then. Now!" Walker rubbed his hands together briskly, to signify a return to business, an end to badinage. "Given all the usual pre-post mortem provisos, get-outs and escape clauses, my initial impressions are as follows. And this incorporates your forensic man's preliminaries, too, since he evidently had somewhere else to be. OK: the deceased—Jones, is it?—Jones died where he was found. The fork blow came from above, while he was prone in the trench, and it was what killed him, though it may have been unnecessary, depending on how he came to be in the trench, and what his general health was like."

"You mean, if he was pushed in there with some force, that might have done for him—eventually, at least? Right...but no bones broken, in fact, as far as you know?"

"So far, inspector. But as I say, I'm pretty confident it was the fork what done 'im in."

"OK," said Don, "so next predictable question is—man or woman?"

"Deceased was a man," Walker replied, straight-faced.

Don laughed dutifully. Then he thought, *Actually, that was quite funny,* so he changed his dutiful laugh to a genuine one, and prolonged it by a few seconds just for fun.

"No, to answer your question, Inspector—could be either. Especially if we guess that he tripped into the trench—perhaps backing away from an attacker, and he does seem quite a slight chap, though not, I would think, particularly frail—then given the angle of the fork blow, it wouldn't have required unusual strength."

"And time of death?"

"Was there a frost this morning?"

"Yes, there was," said Don. "Beautiful, clear morning. Gorgeous morning."

Walker arched an eyebrow. "Indeed? Well. I would say he's been there since, roughly, between eight and ten this morning." The pathologist pulled a notebook out of his coat pocket. "Now then, the forensic notes...Ah yes, I am asked to tell you, in my role as messenger boy, that the murderer would not necessarily be bloodied—an observation with which I concur—and that there are no finger prints on the fork."

"No prints at all?" said Don. "All cleaned off?"

"Gloves, Inspector—that'd be my guess. Gardeners wear gloves when using a garden fork. At this time of year, anyway, and the more sensible types always wear them. To avoid risk of tetanus."

"Of course," said Don. "I see, yes. And how about you, Doc? Do you always wear gloves, like a sensible gardener?"

"Certainly not," the pathologist replied, chortling. "I like to get my hands dirty."

THREE

As WALKER LEFT the site, with one last, longing look back at the purple sprouting, Don went in search of Frank Mitchell.

He liked the lad, he decided, would enjoy working with him. Rather normal, perhaps, rather down to earth in that New Middle Class way that the Force seemed to go in for these days, but bright enough, willing to work, willing to learn. Don got the impression that the young PC, for all his obvious intention to move into plain clothes as soon as possible, was not one of those who gets obsessed about work. The Job to him, was primarily a job. Or rather, a career. It wasn't going to be his whole life.

Well, fair enough. Don himself liked there to be more to his existence than staking out robbers and filling in forms.

He found Frank very much where he'd left him— which was another good sign—sitting on a felt-covered tool box, on the allotment directly opposite Beans's, across the main path. Seated next to him, smoking a roll-up, was a pale, skinny man of about Frank's age, with orange-blond spiky hair and an earring. He was wearing jeans and a T-shirt that looked more shabby than shabby—chic—although not, Don

noted, showing much evidence of garden-induced dirt-
iness.

Frank stood up as Don came aboard the allotment,
and introduced his companion. "This is Mr. Richard
Hancock, sir. This is his plot; he found the body."

"Weed," said Hancock, waving a casual greeting
to the inspector. For a moment Don thought he was
being offered a smoke, but then retrospectively heard
the capital initial.

"That's what they call you, is it? Weed?"

Weed smiled, and flicked his gaze around his allotment. "You can see why, Inspector, I'm sure."

Don could see why. There didn't seem to be any
actual crops growing on the plot at all, unless you
counted the odd stand of what might charitably be
called wild flowers. "You don't go in for beans then,
Weed?"

With a rueful smile, Weed said, "I know what
you're thinking. But no, I don't grow weed here. Honest. Why bother? It's a lot easier just to go down to
the pubs in Hackney once a week and buy it off the
local drug squad. Ho ho." He spoke with minimal jaw
movement, in the manner, it seemed to Don, of most
modern urban youth.

"Ho ho," Don echoed, but he allowed a small smile
to flirt with his lips, briefly. "So, if you don't grow
vegetables and you don't grow dope, allow me to ask
the obvious question: what do you want an allotment
for?"

Weed shrugged. "Just a place to hang, you know?
I live in one room above a pizza joint, the window
looks out on the back wall of a dry cleaner's. Don't
get a lot of air in there, let alone light."

"So you come down here instead."

"Yeah, why not? It's cheap, it's clean, it's pretty. It doesn't smell of dry cleaning chemicals or pepperoni."

"What do you do for a living?" asked Don, settling himself on the other side of the toolbox—a leftover from a previous, more industrious tenant, he assumed. "Or is that a daft question?"

"I'm a bike courier sometimes, when the weather's nice, and I'm unemployed the rest of the time. And no, I don't get the dole, so no need to tell the Social. Ho ho." He said it with a smile, though; Don detected no anti-police hostility from this young man. Or no more than was usual these days, at any rate.

"And what do you do here, when you come down to 'hang'?"

"Sit around, relax, get some sun. Read a book. Chat to people when they feel like chatting. Chat to myself when they don't."

"People don't mind that you're not doing any gardening?"

"Nah, not really. Long as I keep the place reasonably tidy, bung in the occasional row of radishes as a token offering to the god of horticulture. It's like leisure gardens, you know? On the continent?"

"No, I don't know," said Don. "What's a leisure garden? When it's at home?"

"Like Germany and that," said Weed. "I saw it on telly. They have allotments, yeah, but they use them for relaxing in as well as just growing leeks and stuff." He grinned, and had another look round his own patch. "Course, I dare say they go in for it a bit more regimented over there than what I'm doing, but it's the same basic principle.''

"Sounds cool," said Don, raising an eyebrow to show that he was engaged in pastiche, not unconscious self-parody. "And you get on well with the others?''

"Yeah, they're all right," said Weed, taking a last drag on his cigarette and chucking it into a patch of stinging nettles. The gesture, and its accompanying snort of humour, seemed to Don intended to suggest that Weed tolerated the company of his fellow plotters; that they were, needless to say, old and boring, but that he, from his position of cool, youthful superiority, was good enough to humour them with the odd dull exchange.

Don wondered, though, looking at the lad: that *was* loneliness in his eyes, wasn't it? And not just the spring sun?

Don took out his cigars, lit one, offered one to Weed, who declined it with polite thanks. "These nicknames—does everybody have one?''

Weed palmed his locks off his face, and yawned. Why did young people yawn so much these days, Don wondered; were they really so tired all the time, or was it just a fashion thing, like wearing their shirts with the tails on show?

"I don't know, really," said Weed. "I reckon most of them down this end of the site have, yeah. The dead bloke, he was called Beans, yeah? Expect someone's already told you.''

"Where do they come from, then, these names? Is it some official thing? There's a council nicknames committee, is there, attached to the allotments section?''

Weed wheezed a throaty chuckle. "Yeah, like it! Like it, man. Nah—I reckon it was that American woman started it, her with the rejuvenation creams. They go in for all that, don't they, Americans?"

"Which American woman's that?" asked Don.

Frank flipped open his notebook. "Lady by the name of Dill, sir," he said. "Weed has been kind enough to furnish me with a list of all the people who occupy plots at this end of the site; he doesn't know the folk at the other end. And he doesn't know real names, unfortunately, just these nicknames."

"Well, that's fair enough," said Don. "We shall have fun matching people up with their aliases."

"Or we could get a list from the council, sir," Frank suggested.

Yes, thought Don: you like things done the sensible way, don't you? Well, no bad thing in a would-be detective, I suppose.

"Now then, Weed—I understand you found the body. Beans's body."

Weed's smile disappeared, and he rolled another cigarette before answering. "Yeah, right. Thought you'd forgotten to ask me about that."

"We never forget, no," said Don. "We just take our time getting round to things when the sun's shining and the air smells of pollen and new-turned soil."

Weed looked at him sideways, as if the inspector was a bit mad, and as if that were a characteristic to be applauded.

"So," Don continued. "From the start. You went over to Beans's plot, right? Why did you do that?"

Weed reached into a patch of long grass by the tool-box, and produced a sickle. "To give him this. I borrowed it from him a while back. This time of year, even I have to give the weeds a bit of a bash. Otherwise they'll be up to shoulder-height by summer.''

"And spreading their seeds onto your neighbours' plots?" said Frank.

"Right," Weed agreed. "Peaceful coexistence, that's the key to allotment living."

"And what did you see when you stepped on to his land?" asked Don. "Anything odd, anything out of place?"

Weed shook his head, exhaled smoke through his teeth. "No, it was what I didn't see that was odd—didn't see him. No Beans. But I knew he was there, yeah? Because he'd been there when I arrived at sparrowfart this morning, and I knew I hadn't seen him leave."

"You couldn't see the bean trench from where you entered the plot?"

"No. Not that particular one. I mean, he's got more than one trench on the go, yeah? More than one lot of runners. But the one you're talking about, the one where—you know. That one, you can't see it until you're almost on top of it. Because of the shed, and that bloody great compost arrangement, his skyscraper. You've seen that? Made all of pallet wood, you'd think you'd need planning permission for a structure like that. Ho ho."

"So what made you go and have a look in the trench, Weed?"

Weed appeared taken aback by the question. "Nothing! I mean, I didn't go to look at the trench, not as such. I just thought, maybe he was in his shed. Though that would have been a bit odd in itself—like, Beans was pretty much a man of routine, you know? Sundays, he's generally down here all day, and he doesn't go into the shed except to get his tools out when he arrives, put them away when he leaves. And about two o'clock, he'll go in there to smoke his pipe for ten minutes, have a tea from the thermos."

"OK," said Don. "And when you got to the shed…?"

Weed screwed up his face, sucked on his cigarette. "Well, I don't know really. I don't know what it was, I mean. Just…something. Something made me peer into the trench instead of going into the shed. And— well, yeah, you know the rest. There he was. Lying in there, with his fork sticking out of him."

"What did you do? Did you touch him, check if he was dead, anything?"

Weed stood up, breathing in through a tight O between his lips. "I fucking panicked, is what I did, man! I mean—Jesus! I never seen anybody dead before. Jesus! I just—I think I just ran back down the main path, shouting and that."

"What were you shouting?" asked Don. "Do you remember?"

"Nothing very meaningful, I don't suppose," Weed replied, sitting down again. "Just, you know, screaming more or less. Anyway, I didn't stop until I got to that phone booth, the one on the corner of Crockett's Drive, yeah? And I dialled three nines, and that was it."

Don glanced at Frank, to make sure his note taking was keeping up with the narrative. "All right, Weed, that's excellent. Thanks for that. Now, a few more questions. First of all, did you see anyone go onto Beans's plot today? Anyone at all?''

Weed shrugged. "You can see yourself, the way this place is laid out, you spot people coming or going—arriving and leaving, I mean, yeah? Because they've got to take the main path, that's basically the only way of getting around. But as for coming and going between the plots. Well…''

"So what you're saying is it's not something you'd necessarily remember?''

"Right. I could say, no, no one went onto his plot. But—well, obviously someone did, didn't they? I mean, whatever happened there today, it wasn't suicide, was it? Ho ho.''

"And did you see anyone here today who you didn't know? Anyone looking out of place?''

Weed shook his head firmly. "No way. No, now there I can be definite. I am a hundred percent sure that there were no strangers down this end of the site this morning. Not until the two coppers showed up.'' He threw away his cigarette, and immediately started rolling another. "And we all know what that means, don't we?''

Don ignored the last comment. "Right, now this is the same question, basically, but I just want to make sure. You didn't *hear* anything, or anyone, either? Because, it seems to me—''

"That he didn't die silent,'' Weed interrupted. "Yeah, same thought struck me. Poor old sod must've… well, anyway, when I thought back on it, it's not actually much of a mystery.''

"No?''

Weed pointed towards the allotment immediately

below the dead man's (literally below, since the site sloped slightly towards the road). "That one belongs to Queer Gear, and—"

"Queer Gear?" said Frank. "Who's he?"

"She," said Weed. "Some old girl, she's a writer or something. Anyway, point is, she was using a rotovator all morning. Hired it specially, turn over the soil before the big planting season begins."

"And it makes a noise?"

"Hell of a noise. Give me a headache, in fact. Still, live and let live, eh?"

"A rotovator was going all morning, right next to where the murder took place," said Don. "Well, thanks, Weed, that does explain a lot."

"Welcome."

"Tell me about old Beans. What was he like? Nice enough old guy, was he?"

"Yeah, he was all right. Don't suppose he approved of me, or my allotment, but he never gave me any crap over it."

"Talkative? Friendly?"

"Not talkative exactly, no. Bit, you know, tight-lipped really. Kept his own counsel, sort of thing."

"But you did talk with him occasionally?" said Don. "Like when you borrowed his tools?"

"Oh yeah, he was as nice as anything about that, you know—not mean at all. As long you took care of things. And he was generous with his produce. Well, you know, all those beans, he could hardly get through them all on his own, could he?"

"And what sort of things did you talk about, when you talked?"

"Like I say, he wasn't your actual chatterbox, not

by any means. But he'd pass the time of day, yeah.
Allotment stuff. That's a sort of rule down here; nobody really talks about the outside world at all. I think
it's like pubs, you know, you sometimes see those
signs behind the bar: no politics or religion. Like, if
you just talk about the specific thing you've got in
common, the allotments, you won't get into any arguments or anything. Well, people come down here to
get away from the world, don't they? They don't want
to bring it with them.''

Don saw that Frank was nodding, perhaps uncon-
sciously, in agreement.

With a friendly smile, Don said, ''That didn't leave
you two much to talk about, though, did it? What with
you not actually doing any gardening?''

''Oh, you'd be surprised. It's not all carrots and
slugs on the allotments, you know. We talk about the
weather, and the wildlife and that. You get some
amazing wildlife on the allotments, you wouldn't believe it. You'd think you were out in the countryside,
some of the things you see here.''

''It sounds idyllic,'' said Don, and he meant it. It
did: it sounded perfect. You could hardly hear the traf-
fic from here, and the slight road rumble you could
hear only served to emphasise its remoteness. Closing
his eyes for a moment, just for a second, he could,
indeed, imagine himself in the middle of the country.
Or, perhaps, in some even more exotic location: an
island in a green sea, a kingdom of treetops, a garden
exempt from time. A million miles from work and
struggle, at any rate.

He could smell a dozen different plants, though he
couldn't guess what they were—some green, some flo-

ral, some stinking of earth and root. He could hear a dozen different insects buzzing and whining, and birds flapping and gliding.

And this was only spring, sweet, unreliable spring, that gardener's tease! Imagine what high summer must be like... Get this murder sorted out, perhaps he'd take on Beans's plot himself. Ah, well: later. He opened his eyes. "Did Beans seem happy to you, when you spoke to him?"

The question obviously baffled Weed. "Happy? He was old."

Don couldn't help laughing at that. "Yes, point taken. But what I mean is, recently, did there seem to be anything bothering him, especially? Apart from the general despair of having one foot in the grave, let's say."

"Ho ho," said Weed. "Nah, not really, not that I particularly noticed. He was a bit pissed off about the Allotment Society, I suppose."

"Why was that?" asked Frank.

"Well, I don't know, really. They've got this society, you know, you pay a couple of quid a year or something and you can get, like, cheap fertilisers and that."

"And Beans ran it?" Frank guessed.

"Right. And I gather it used to be quite a big deal, annual dinner and cups for the best turnips and what have you. Only I reckon this lot, the others, weren't all that interested."

"So Beans felt the current generation of plotters was letting him down? Not pulling their weight?"

"Something like that, maybe. And, yeah, now I

come to think of it, he called some big meeting about it a while back.''

''And what happened there?''

Weed wrinkled his nose. ''You'll have to ask someone else. Not really my thing, you know—meetings?''

''I'm sure,'' said Don, his senses still buzzing from his quick trip to the Garden That Time Forgot. ''You had enough of all that when you were chairman of ICI, right?''

''Right,'' said Weed, laughing now—a giggly, uncontrolled sound, in contrast to the measured irony of his ho-hos. ''That was before I dropped out of the rat race to find myself.''

Don glanced at Frank, thinking—same generation, different planet. This boy here had almost certainly never had a proper job, and almost certainly never would. And he didn't think that situation sufficiently extraordinary to warrant more than a spot of witty dialogue. Whereas Frank, going by the expression on his face, wasn't even a hundred per cent sure what the joke was.

''So, Weed,'' said Don, standing up and stretching his arms above his head. ''By the sound of it, you have no idea whatsoever who might have wanted to hurt old Beans?''

Weed shook his head, gravely. ''I have not.''

''Not necessarily kill him, even, but hurt him— threaten him, scare him?''

''I have not,'' said Weed. ''One of them's done this, but I can't for the life of me imagine why.''

OVER LUNCH in a reasonably inoffensive local pub— good bottled beer, grated cheese sandwiches, taped

Beatles medley suppressed by loud air conditioning—Don said: "He catches on quick, that lad, doesn't he?"

"You mean the 'one of them' remark? Yes, I noticed that too."

Don nodded, pushed his plate away and lit a cigar. "Yes, that. And also earlier, when he said something about 'We all know what that means, don't we.' And he's right isn't he?" From behind the smoke, Don peered sideways at Frank, excitement and anticipation dancing in the creases around his eyes.

"That the killer is someone on this list?" said Frank, tapping the notebook in his jacket pocket. "It certainly looks like that, doesn't it? Depending on what the other plotters tell us, of course, but if it's true that a stranger on the site would be noticed, and that no such stranger *was* noticed... Well, subject to confirmation of time and place of death, I'd say—"

Don laughed, choked on his cigar smoke, waved away Frank's offer of a pat on the back. "You wouldn't say anything that might be taken down and used against you later, Frank, would you?" He had a few tears in his eyes; whether from mirth or choking, Frank wasn't sure.

"Sorry if you think I'm being negative, sir," he said, consciously trying to relax his voice, not to sound wooden or huffy. "I'm just the sort of person, I like to know where I'm going and what I'm doing." I like things worked out properly, he thought; but I wouldn't say I was obsessive about it.

"No, don't apologise, Frank," said Don. "Methodical is good; step by step, that's the proper CID way." He finished his beer. "It even works, sometimes."

FOUR

COMPARING THE TWO LISTS—the list of witnesses taken by PC Standfield, and the list of nicknames supplied by Weed—they decided that Dill, Weed's "American woman," must surely be Leonora Daniels.

"Sounds American," Don had said. "Don't you reckon?"

As Ms. Daniels opened the door to them at her smart semi in a quiet road about five minutes walk from the allotments, she confirmed their guess with her mild, modulated, but unmistakably North American accent.

Frank thought he would have spotted her for an American even if she hadn't spoken. Looking somewhere in her forties (though from Standfield's details he knew she was actually 55), she had the straight, white teeth traditionally associated with that part of the world, expensive-looking hair of a vaguely blond colour, and the sharp, assertive, almost resentful facial expression which, his viewing of TV had taught him, all middle-class American women perennially wear.

Dill served tea to the two policemen in her living room. It was furnished, Frank thought, in a way that showed there was no shortage of money. But the effect was slightly cold, more like a place of business than of residence.

Frank sat on the edge of a suite chair, while Don looked out through the French windows onto a decent-sized, but, to his inexpert eye, somewhat under-exploited garden.

"You have a nice patch of garden of your own, Ms. Daniels," he said, as she poured the tea. "I'm surprised you have time for an allotment on top of that."

"I'm a widow, Inspector," she replied. "It can get a bit lonely. The allotment provides a social outlet as well as a horticultural one."

"Of course," said Don. "I understand. The gardening is only part of the reason people take on a plot, isn't it? I'm beginning to see that." He sat on the sofa and sipped his tea. "One thing we're trying to get clear in our minds, Ms. Daniels. Is it possible that a stranger could have—"

"No," she said, shaking her head firmly.

"You were all busy with your various tasks," Don continued, "isn't it perhaps—"

"No," she said again, insistently. "Look. We've had a certain amount of trouble in the past with intruders. All allotment sites do to some extent or another, and the council doesn't do a damn thing about it. So we all keep our eyes open. Anyone who doesn't belong is challenged—you can count on that."

"When you say intruders," said Frank, "are you referring to vandalism?"

"Not only vandalism," she said. "Yes, we do get some mindless damage now and then—graffiti on the sheds, crops dug up and left to rot on the ground. The usual sort of stuff. But more importantly, there are outbreaks of theft."

"Of *what?*" said Don, and Frank guessed that his

boss was grappling with a mental image of a stripey-shirted burglar filling his swag bag with prize swedes.

"Some allotmenteers keep their tools in their sheds, or in lock-up boxes," explained Dill. "You'd perhaps be surprised, but the value of some of those items of equipment can really mount up." She sipped her tea, and muttered *That's nice,* as if she were the guest not the hostess. "And then, of course, there are the grazers, Inspector."

"Grazers?" asked Don, as he was obviously meant to.

She nodded, and attached a wry smile to her lips. "That's what I call them. I couldn't believe it the first time I saw one. I hadn't had my allotment long—I've been there about eighteen months now—and I was digging out some couch grass, when I happened to look up and see, on the plot across the path from mine, someone eating blackberries straight from the bush."

"Someone whose plot it wasn't, you mean?"

"Sure. I knew the person who gardened there—a Hispanic guy—and this was a fat, white woman, wearing a headscarf. And as I watched, I saw that not only was she eating the berries, she was filling a Tupperware box with them too! So I went over and said, like, *Excuse me*—and do you know, she was utterly unrepentant."

"Really?" said Don, impressing Frank with the way his tone managed to suggest that, hardened copper or not, he was deeply shocked by such naked criminality.

"Oh, you better believe it, Inspector! She said, *'Well blackberries grow wild, don't they?'* But I mean, we're not talking some kind of bramble in a hedgerow—these were proper blackberry canes, carefully trained and everything." She shook her head. "Some people!"

"Indeed," said Don, sadly. "So now you all keep a pretty close eye on comings and goings on the site?"

"We do," said Dill. "There's no actual right of way for the public across the allotments, but that doesn't stop people trying to exercise their shitting dogs there. And the council's too stingy to fork out for a gate that locks. So—yes, we are vigilant. Though obviously that's easier when there's a lot of us there. Weekends and so on, sunny days."

"And this morning, was there a good turn-out?"

"Oh yes, I'd say pretty much a full turn-out, right from breakfast time. Down our end of the site, anyhow."

"In which case, you could say with some confidence that there were no strangers on the allotments today?"

"With complete confidence, Inspector. Yes." Her face hardened, and she put down her tea cup. "And since I'm not an idiot, I do know what that means. Or rather, what I'm sure it means to you."

Don sat back in his chair and crossed his legs. "Ah. And what does it mean to you, Ms. Daniels?"

"This, Inspector. That old Beans's death must most surely have been an accident."

"Didn't look very accidental," said Frank.

She glanced at him briefly, and then returned her attention to his superior. "Contrary to what people think, gardening can be a pretty dangerous activity. There are statistics, you know. People—especially old people—can become careless. It is truly very easy indeed to have an accident, a serious accident, on an allotment. Sharp tools, uneven ground, canes to poke out your eyes…I take my safety very seriously, Inspector, but sometimes older people, well, they like to do things their own way.''

"All right, Ms. Daniels," said Don. "Good point. And until we have the results of all our tests, we can't say for sure that you're not right. But just supposing it was murder. And, as we've established, that murder must have been committed by one of your fellow plotters. Can you think of a motive at all?''

"Well…" said Dill, fiddling with her now empty cup.

"I'm not asking you to point any fingers, you understand. Just to suggest a reason—anything—the smallest disagreement between Beans and another gardener, which might conceivably have turned violent. You see," he added, as Dill began to speak, "none of you really has an alibi, as such. You were all there; you all had the means. Which leaves us with motive, alone, to help us in the process of elimination.''

Dill nodded to herself for a while, gazing down at her lap. Then she raised her eyes to meet Don's, as if she had made up her mind to perform a painful duty. Or rather, Frank thought, as if that was what she wanted to seem to be doing.

"This may sound a little far-fetched, Inspector," she began. "I don't know how much you know about the allotment scene.''

"Absolutely nothing," said Don, cheerfully. "But my young colleague here is a leading expert on the subject.''

Dill didn't even glance at Frank this time, but acknowledged Don's words with a fast, thin, on/off smile. "The thing is, Inspector, allotment gardening arouses passions which would probably seem extraordinary to an outsider."

"Much like any special interest," said Don.

"No, that's my point, you see. Allotments are about *land*. It's not just another hobby, like stamp collecting or hang-gliding. It's about land, and that makes it almost primal. You're familiar with the history of the allotment movement?"

"Oh, certainly," said Don. *Liar,* thought Frank.

"Then you'll understand that what people are doing when they rent an allotment—taking on a piece of land that is measured in such archaic units as rods and poles and perch—is they're reclaiming their right to till the soil. A right which was denied to them by the enclosures and by the industrial revolution. It goes way deeper than parsnips and gooseberries, Inspector, it goes all the way back to—"

"I take your point, Ms. Daniels, yes indeed I do. And I confess, I hadn't looked at it quite like that before. But, well, land alienation and the theory of the urban peasant aside; I'm not sure it gets us very much further forward."

There was a brief, blinking silence, while the other two people in the room made certain that their faces did not betray astonishment at the ease with which Detective Inspector Packham had one-upped Leonora Daniels's high falution.

And then, in Frank's view, Don had to go and spoil it all: "Or are you suggesting, Ms. Daniels, that we should be seeking to interview the Sheriff of Nottingham?"

Dill laughed. "No. What I am suggesting is that, if there was indeed a murder, then it is likely to have its roots in certain matters of land ownership with which you may not yet be acquainted."

"Land ownership?" said Frank, a determination growing in him that Lady Dill should be forced to honour him with a response sooner or later. "But surely the land's owned by the council."

"So it is, of course," Dill replied, her eyes not straying from the DI's face. "Local authorities are legally obliged to provide space for allotments, if there's local demand, under the Allotment Act of—"

"1908," said Don. He followed this smooth interruption with an undisguised matey wink at Frank. "Section 23, I fancy."

"Quite so," said Dill, who did now turn her head to look at Frank, but only fleetingly, as if to wonder what he thought he was doing there. "But as you may also know, Inspector—since your knowledge of the law is clearly encyclopaedic—the legislation is somewhat vague. And, naturally, in the present political climate, loosely-interpreted and half-heartedly enforced laws are scarcely sufficient to stand against well-organised and well-funded commercial interests."

Funny, thought Frank; wouldn't have had her down as a leftie. Rather the opposite.

"But," he said, as he realised that she had paused for breath, "the land is owned by the council, yes?"

She sighed impatiently, and raised her eyebrows at Don. "*Yes,* obviously the land is *owned* by the council."

"In which case I'm sorry, but I don't quite understand your point,'' said Frank. There are times, he thought, when stubbornness is no sin.

"My point,'' said Dill, addressing Don, "is that there are plans afoot to sell off the Crockett's Drive allotment site. To sell it, that is, to developers, who will build upon it business units and supermarkets and car parks and luxury dwellings and, for all I know, nuclear power stations and missile silos. You see?''

"And it is in this threat, you suggest, where we will find the motive for the death of old Beans?'' said Don. Frank was impressed: Throughout the woman's ramblings, Don had worn such an expression of studied concentration that Frank had assumed he wasn't listening. Now it turned out that not only had he been listening, he had even managed to follow her train of thought.

"That's it, Inspector. Told you it would sound far-fetched,'' said Dill, with a coy smile.

"Not at all, Ms. Daniels,'' Don assured her. "Where big money's involved, there's always likely to be crime lurking in the shadows.''

"Well, exactly.'' She leaned forward enthusiastically. "And we are talking big money here, believe me. Big money, and big corruption.''

"Corruption, Ms. Daniels?'' said Don, his tone slightly cooler. Never a CID man's favourite word, thought Frank.

"Oh yes, Inspector. Corruption. I don't doubt it for a moment. The links between some of these local councillors and the businessmen involved in the development scheme—well, they would repay closer scrutiny, let us put it like that. I shouldn't wonder if they were all members of the same lodge, shouldn't wonder at all.''

"I'm not sure membership of the Freemasons would, on its own, provide sufficient evidence to convince the CPS to bring a charge of murder against person or persons unknown," said Don. "Not even if they are every bit as corrupt as you suspect them to be.''

"You mean, where's my proof?'' Dill's smile was smug, as were her crossed arms and arched eyebrows. As if she were doing "smug" in a game of charades, thought Frank. "I don't have any proof, of course," she admitted. "But then, if you remember, Inspector, it was you who insisted that poor old Mr. Jones had been murdered. I'm still sticking out for accidental death.''

"Ha! Quite right, Ms. Daniels. Quite right. You've got me there. But I do see one rather significant objection to the Death By Freemasonry scenario, in any case. And that is that we are still left with no strangers having been seen on the site at the relevant time. Now of course it may be that when we subsequently speak to the rest of your fellow plotters, one or more of them may, after all, have spotted an intruder. But, assuming that is not the case…''

Dill narrowed her lips, and placed a finger against them, in a gesture that seemed to Frank half way between *"Shh!"* and *"Let us pray."*

"I do take your point, Inspector, yes. Well, all I can say is, without in any way accepting the idea for so much as a moment that any of my allotment neighbours could possibly have been involved in anything like this at all—''

"That's the longest proviso I've heard in months," Don muttered.

Ignoring him, Dill continued, "All I can say is that opinion amongst the allotmenteers is not entirely unanimous on the development question. There has been talk of compensation, you understand."

"You mean some of the plot-holders are actually in favour of selling out? I see. Would you like to tell us which ones?"

"It's not quite that simple, Inspector. There was a meeting a week or so ago, attended by most of the allotmenteers—"

"Ah, yes," Don interrupted. "Convened by Beans, I understand?"

"Well, yes, technically I guess."

"Technically?"

Dill cleared her throat delicately. "Mr. Jones is—was—the chairman of the Crockett's Drive Allotment Society. Therefore, the notice of the meeting went out under his name."

"But you're telling us, Ms. Daniels, that he was not in reality the main moving spirit behind the initiative?"

"Well—"

"Or does modesty forbid, Ms. Daniels?"

"I have certainly involved myself, since taking up an allotment on the site, in ensuring that we are able to offer a vigorous and effective opposition to these disgraceful plans. It is essential, Inspector, that community resources like allotments are safeguarded for future generations."

"Quite right," said Don. "I'm sure PC Mitchell's

grandfather would join in those sentiments too, isn't that right, Frank?''

''If he wasn't dead, sir, yes.''

''But if you, and not Beans, represent the main focus of resistance to the development plans, then why should a supporter of those plans kill him? Why not kill you?''

''*If* he was killed,'' said Dill, ''then perhaps it was simply because he was the nominal leader of the Society. Or perhaps, given his well-known interest in local history—you knew about that?—they feared that he had, or would, uncover something damaging to their cause. An ancient by-law, or charter, or something.''

''So tell me about these magic potions of yours, Ms. Daniels,'' Don said, in a sudden change of direction which left Dill blinking. And reddening, Frank noted; yes, definitely a certain colouring of the cheeks there.

''Magic potions, Inspector?'' she said.

''One of your friends on the site mentioned something about—what was it, PC Mitchell? Beauty preparations?''

''Something in that line, sir, I believe,'' said Frank, who vaguely recollected Weed's throwaway comment, but couldn't imagine why the DI should have thought it worth catching.

Still, no doubt about it, he thought, spotting Dill's irritated swipe at her fringe: she really wasn't keen to discuss this.

''I have an interest in herbal cosmetics. Perhaps that's what you mean.''

''That'll be it,'' Don agreed, cheerfully. ''Tell us about that.''

"Just a hobby, Inspector. I use my allotment for growing herbs, and I enjoy experimenting with them, trying out old recipes and so on. I can't imagine that is of great interest to the police, surely?"

Well, fair play, she did look pretty good for her age, thought Frank. If you went for that sort.

"Just a hobby, then?" said Don, apparently immune to the frosty atmosphere. "Not a commercial undertaking at all?"

"Oh, hardly commercial!" she protested, with an unconvincing snort of laughter.

"You don't sell your preparations? What are they—face creams, that sort of thing?"

"That sort of thing, Inspector, yes. I could be more specific, but—no offence—I think I'd be wasting my time and yours. I've yet to meet a man who could tell a moisturiser from a skin toner."

"Nor have you met one in me, I'm afraid," said Don. "And these are just for personal use? You're not starting a cottage industry?"

"Have I broken some sort of archaic licensing law, Inspector?"

"Wouldn't interest us if you had, Ms. Daniels. Not our department. But you do sell them, then?"

Suddenly, Frank got the impression that the DI was so relentlessly pursuing this presumably irrelevant line of questioning purely because his questionee was so relentlessly retreating from it.

Dill waved a hand in front of her face, as if shooing a fly. "I occasionally take a stall at a market. Camden Lock, somewhere like that. Not what you could call commercial, not in the sense you mean. A hobby, Inspector, as I said."

"Fine," said Don, getting to his feet. "We'll be off, then. Thanks for the tea."

Frank fumbled his notebook into his pocket and stood also. Dill took a little longer to rise, evidently taken aback at the abruptness with which the interview had been terminated.

"I hope you don't think I'm being wilfully obstructive, Inspector—reluctant to answer your questions, I mean. It's just that, well…" She raised her eyebrows in what Frank supposed was meant to be a self-deprecating mannerism. "I am an American, after all. I find that this European habit of discussing other people's business so openly takes a little getting used to."

"Not to worry, Ms. Daniels," said Don. "I like my privacy, too—no crime in that."

But the two detectives were hardly out of earshot before Don muttered to his colleague, "What do you reckon? Think she killed the old bloke to get leadership of the Allotment Society?"

"I suppose it's not impossible, sir," said Frank, doubtfully.

"Either that," said Don, "or it could be the first recorded case of Allotment Rage."

FIVE

"So what's he like? Your Mr. Packham?"

Debbie Mitchell, pregnant with their first child, had given up her nursing job as soon as her instincts told her that resigning would not be considered hubristic by any of the various gods in whom she did not believe.

And she was enjoying the break, this lull between exhausting work and exhausting motherhood. Debbie did not come from the sort of background where women undertook paid employment in order to "define their identities" or to "establish their space as an individual"—was not one of them, and had no sympathy for them.

One thing she did miss from work, though: not the hours, not the pay, not the being treated like shit by politicians, managers and, not infrequently, patients. She missed the gossip. Not the girly gossip, not the boyfriends and make-up stuff. More the focused gossip—idle chat between people in the same line of work, with the same experiences, using the same jargon, making the same connections.

Unfortunately, she could not even enjoy this pleasure vicariously. Frank was not a great talker about work, and they had always tended to socialise more with hospital friends than with cop-shop friends.

Her husband was a great believer in clocking off. He had been attracted to the police service as a career, or at least as a long-term job, by the pay, the security, the pension, the benefits, the opportunity to get on. He hadn't joined in order to save the world, or, conversely, for an excuse to kick folk's heads in and scrounge free meals at Indian restaurants.

He took his duties seriously, she knew that, as he took all his duties seriously, including husband, mortgage-payer, father-to-be...even washer-up and setter-of-the-video-recorder. He believed in an ethos of fairness and public service, and was constantly, quietly, aware of the need to live up to it.

But it was a job, that was the point: a job, not a life.

When he came home, and sat next to Debbie on their buy-now-pay-later sofa in front of a muted TV set: *this* was his life.

Even so, she couldn't help asking, "So what's he like? Isn't he the one Dave Gittings was going on about in the pub, last Christmas?"

Frank settled himself deeper into the sofa, and deeper into his wife's embrace. Bloody good sofa, this. His mum had gone green when she saw it; better than anything they'd had when he was a kid.

"I don't know really," he said, after a moment's thought. "He seems OK, really. Friendly bloke, informal—wants me to call him Don. Yeah, he's fine."

"So what's all this monster reputation about, then? All this *keep away from that'un, lad, 'e be trouble* stuff?"

"Who knows?" said Frank, on a yawn. "Stupid canteen gossip, most likely. Who cares?"

WHEN HE ARRIVED at the station on Monday morning, the day after the discovery of Arthur Jones's body, Frank went straight to the locker room to change from his uniform into plain clothes. Attached to his locker there was a note, written by DI Packham and dated the previous evening, telling Frank to meet him at a particular pub near the allotment site; not the one they'd been in yesterday lunchtime. "This one opens at 7 a.m. for breakfast," Don had written.

Frank had never had breakfast in a pub—unless you counted a plate full of cheese rolls at eleven o'clock on a Saturday morning, after a heavy bevvy the previous evening—and he wasn't sure the idea appealed greatly.

Still, he'd had breakfast before he left for work (one advantage of having a non-working wife), and a cup of tea wouldn't hurt. Drinking tea in a pub, eh? By God, they were living in interesting times!

It didn't look as if the DI had arrived with much of an appetite either, considering that the only thing on the table in front of him, in the darkest, furthest corner of the vast, barn-like pub, was an untouched cup of tea, its individual, tagged tea bag still in situ.

"Morning, Don," said Frank as he took the chair next to his boss. "Have you eaten, then?"

Don's response was a dark, sideways glance, and a grunt.

Oh shit, thought Frank. I shouldn't have called him Don. Just because he says I'm to, doesn't mean he means it.

He went up to the bar to get himself a cup of coffee (the tea couldn't be up to much, if Don hadn't even tried his). They sat in silence for a while on his return to the table, until even Frank, who did not consider himself overly sensitive, felt he couldn't stand the quiet any longer.

"Strange this, isn't it, sir? Sitting in a pub at this time of day. No booze anywhere, I mean—just the smell of beer left over from last night. Hardly any customers. No juke box, no tobacco smoke, no darts match, no—"

"What?" Don snapped, as if Frank had interrupted him in the middle of a long-distance phone call.

"Nothing, sir," Frank replied, thinking: What the hell's got into him? What have I done wrong? This can't all be because I called him Don. Or is it nothing to do with me, nothing to do with the Job; has something happened at home? He realised that he knew nothing of the DI's private life, either from direct conversation with the man himself, or from gossip.

He made a few more half-hearted attempts to establish verbal communication—Christ, even a moment of eye contact would be something!—before finally deciding that, whatever the cause of Mr. Packham's catatonia, if it was left to the DI they'd still be sat here staring at the carpet when the lunchtime crowd arrived.

Frank would have to take the lead. Nothing else for it; first full day as an apprentice detective, and he was going to have to assume command. Fair enough: no one had ever accused Frank Mitchell of being a ditherer.

"I imagine we'll be wanting to see some more of the plotters this morning, sir?" No response, so he ploughed on. "How about this Daphne Lender, next? Gave her occupation as writer, so I guess she must be the one that Weed calls Queer Gear, yeah?"

"Bloody stupid," Don muttered, and Frank had no idea whether he meant Weed, the nicknames, Frank's suggested course of action—or the whole investigation.

Or maybe just life, the universe and everything.

Well, I'm not just sitting still for this, he told himself. OK, so Don's had a row with his wife, that's no reason to take it out on me.

"Right then," he said, standing up. "Shall we go, sir?"

"What?" said Don. Frank wondered if the miserable sod even knew who he was talking to. Does he remember leaving that note on my locker? Does he remember working with me yesterday? Does he speak English?

"The lady writer, sir. Daphne Lender. Should be good for a bit of loose talk, I would have thought—a writer. Maybe she'll be able to tell us who had it in for poor old Beans."

THEY FOUND Miss Lender at home in her small, unfussy bungalow on the outskirts of the allotment site's catchment area. Frank introduced himself and Don, and showed his warrant card. Don didn't show his; just stood there behind Frank, hands in pockets, eyes unfocussed, like an idiot child.

His behaviour drew a puzzled look from Daphne Lender, as she sat them down in the living room. Frank decided that a flow of conversation would be the best way of distracting her.

"Sorry to disturb you at your work, Miss Lender," he said. "Must be difficult when you work at home, people dropping in unannounced at every hour of the day.''

She laughed. ''On the contrary, Constable, any excuse to break off from the dreaded blank page for a moment is avidly seized upon! I don't get nearly enough interruptions, to tell you the truth. This isn't exactly a dropping-in sort of neighbourhood.''

Frank studied her through the kitchen doorway (from which vantage point he could also keep a paternal eye on the Problem Child) as she prepared the inevitable tray of coffee and biscuits. She was in her late forties; hair brushed rather than coiffured and mostly grey; not a lot of make-up, simple, casual clothes—skirt, blouse, jumper, flat shoes. Nice-looking woman; not attractive, in the sexual sense, but she looked like good company—open, kind, humorous.

Quite possibly a murderer, too, of course.

''So what sort of stuff do you write?'' asked Frank, as she returned to the living room. He said it as if he was interested, but hoped her reply would be a brief one.

''Ah, well now,'' she said in what he reckoned was an Edinburgh accent. ''That, I'm afraid, is something of a sore point.''

''Oh, indeed?'' Out of the corner of his eye he could see Don bent over the steaming mug he held cupped in both hands, alternately blowing on its surface and staring into its depths, like a *Screen Two* version of a down-and-out.

He was careful not to look at Don full-face, in case the woman's gaze followed his.

''Yes,'' she said, running her fingers through her

hair. "I write what is rather absurdly known as *literary fiction.*"

"Ah," said Frank; he knew what 'literary' meant. "And it doesn't sell?"

Her eyes opened wide. "No, it does sell—that's just the problem! It sells far too well, so that my agent and my publisher and not forgetting my accountant won't let me write anything else. I started straight from university, you see, and, like most young, over-educated, would-be writers who have not lived long enough to have anything to write about, I turned to that old stand-by, literary obfuscation and experimentation. Purely for the purpose of getting something, anything, down on paper, you understand?"

"Oh yes," said Frank, wondering what she was on about.

"Tragically, as it turned out, my juvenilia was not only published, but was picked up by one particular—and particularly pseudy-critic, and became a minor sensation. Well, from there on I was trapped. My fate was sealed; my direction unchangeable."

"You could have got a job in the civil service, I suppose," Frank suggested, thinking of a cousin of his who had gone to university, and was currently something quite senior in the Department of the Environment.

Again, she widened her eyes. Frank recognised the mime, second time round: it meant, Gosh! Aren't you a blunt-speaking chap! How jolly refreshing!

"I could, of course," she replied, "always supposing they would have found a niche for a specialist in the eighteenth century novel. But you see, Mr. Mitchell, I did—I *do*—want to be a writer. I just don't want to be the writer I am."

"But you make a decent living, anyway?" said Frank, who tended to reserve his sympathy for slightly more obvious cases of vile oppression.

"Yes, can't grumble about the wages; good point, Constable. It's a myth that snob fiction doesn't sell. How could it fail to do so, when every newspaper, radio and TV show in the country promotes it so incessantly? The Establishment safety net, I call it—it's our equivalent of the farmers' EEC subsidy, and just as unearned. Oh yes, people buy my books. They don't read them, but they buy them."

No, be fair, Frank corrected himself. She's not after sympathy; she's just glad of an opportunity to flap her lips. Well, let's get 'em good and flappy and see what comes out.

"So what sort of stuff would you write, if you had your own way?"

She placed a hand in front of her mouth, as if she'd just let out a ladylike burp. "Detective fiction, I fear. I don't imagine that is a confession likely to win one many constabulary admirers."

"Oh, I don't know so much," said Frank, smiling generously. "Case like this one, Mr. Jones's suspicious death, we can do with all the help we can get. So, please feel free to point us in the right direction, Miss Marple. Or," he added, twirling an imaginary Belgian moustache with his fingertips, "should I call you…Miss Queer Gear!"

Queer Gear shook with delighted giggles, to the point where Frank wondered if her teeth were going to fall out, and hoped she wouldn't sue if they did.

"Ah, Monsieur Poirot, so you have solved the mystery of the plot nicknames, I see! Excellent—but do you know *why* they call me Queer Gear?"

"One hardly likes to ask," said Frank. He was enjoying this. Half of his mind was aware that the other half had quite forgotten about old Don Packham.

"It's a term used in the greengrocery trade," she explained. "Used both in wholesale and in retail, I believe, and it refers to exotic produce—fruits and vegetables that are stocked for the more discerning shopper, things which are without the normal run of potatoes, leeks and cabbages."

"And this is the kind of stuff you grow on your allotment?"

"I do indeed," she said. The more enthusiastically she spoke, the more Scots her voice became, Frank noticed; and wondered if the same applied to his Geordie accent. "I find gardening fascinating, very relaxing, very rewarding. Best thing I ever did, taking on an allotment, Mr. Mitchell, especially with a job like mine. You know—solitary, indoors, concentrated. But I soon got bored with growing the same old crops as everyone else. The same old crops that I could just as easily buy from the supermarket. So I experiment. I'll have a go at anything, anything at all, provided it sounds a bit, well, *queer*. Half of the things I grow I bet you'd never even have heard of."

Frank searched his memory for the peculiar words he'd heard his granddad use, twenty years ago...odd, foreign sounds which had fascinated him as a child. "Scorzonera?" he said.

Queer Gear's delight was so great this time that she seemed hardly able to stay in her chair. "Scorzonera!

One of my absolute favourites! You are a man of depths, Mr. Mitchell—and please notice, I do not say hidden depths, for I've always thought that to be a somewhat double-edged compliment at best.''

"So tell me," said Frank. "What did Arthur Jones think of your choice of crops? They called him Beans, didn't they, so I don't imagine he was much of a one for the exotics?''

The writer settled her face into a suitably sombre expression. "Ah, that's a terrible thing, someone killing that poor old man. I'm quite sure he'd never done anyone a bit of harm in all his days. Though I suppose that's a daft idea, really; we're all capable of cruelty at times, no doubt.''

"But you never saw any evidence of cruelty in Beans?''

"Never at all." She hesitated. "Despite what we were saying earlier, please do tell me if I'm teaching my grandmother to suck eggs.''

"Go on.''

"Well, I'm sure by now you've had a chance to study the layout of the site, yes? And the habits and concerns of the plotholders. So you'll have come to the same conclusion as I, which is that you are dealing with, shall we say, a limited circle of suspects?''

"It does seem probable," said Frank, carefully, "that Mr. Jones was killed by someone who has an allotment at Crockett's Drive.''

"Oh! I see there is a minor point of egg-sucking on which I might legitimately offer you advice, Constable. You see, the list is even more restricted than that.''

"It is? How so?''

"Well now, let me see if I am second-guessing you correctly. You have already learned that we have experienced certain problems on the site from unwelcome visitors, and that therefore we plotters tend to be vigilant—that is, to keep an eye open for strangers. Right so far, Mr. Mitchell?"

"Correct," said Frank.

"Since, therefore, you have heard no reports of unidentified persons being present on the allotments on the morning in question—"

"An observation which you would confirm?"

"Oh yes," said Queer Gear. "I am quite certain that no one was abroad that day who should not have been."

"Thank you." Frank made a note in his pad.

"On this basis, therefore, you conclude that whoever attacked poor old Beans must have been one of his fellow plotholders."

"Right," said Frank.

"Right. But, as I say, the list can reasonably be reduced further. You see, Beans's allotment is situated at what we refer to as the 'Tap End' of the site."

Examining his mental picture of the scene, Frank said, "But there are taps at both ends."

Queer Gear smiled. "Quite so. The appellation is, you understand, an ironic one. You see, the taps run in series, the water being drawn from a main on the road. Thus, when the tap is run at the gate end—or Gate End, with capital initials, as we call it—the tap at our end loses pressure. Hence, Tap End—meaning the end at which we poor, underprivileged toilers suffer from an intermittently inadequate water supply."

"I follow you," said Frank. "Please go on."

"Now then. You will have observed that the two halves of the site—approximate halves, I mean—are divided by a large shed. In times when the Allotment Society was a more thriving concern than it has been of late, that was a sort of general store, from which discounted seeds, fertilisers and so on were sold to members. It's still used occasionally as a meeting place."

"I see," said Frank, remembering his granddad's plot, and beginning to guess where she was heading.

"Yes, I'm sure you do. This shed, and the business of the taps, seem to reinforce what is, I suppose, a natural disposition towards tribalism within human society."

"You're saying you don't have much to do with the Gate Enders?" said Frank.

"Precisely so. Whereas I am on at least nodding terms with all ten of my fellow tenants at the Tap End—nine I should say, with Beans's demise—I have never had anything much to do with those foreign devils, with their strange customs and barbaric ways, who huddle in the sunless regions of the Land of Gate! An entirely baseless and purposeless piece of clannishness, no doubt, but one which is not, I would say, unusual wherever three or more Sons of Adam or Daughters of Eve are gathered together."

Frank picked the meat out of Queer Gear's literary soup, and then said, "In other words, when Tap Enders tell us that they saw no strangers on the site that morning, they don't just mean non-plotters—"

"We also mean," she interrupted with an emphatic nod, "that we can say, with a high degree of certainty, that if anyone from the Gate End had wandered on to our territory we should most definitely have noted their presence.''

Frank risked a glance at the DI; this was, surely, a significant piece of information. If true, it did, as Queer Gear claimed, reduce the list of suspects to a mere ten. But Don gave no sign of having heard the conversation. His shoulders were still down, his face still dead.

Damn it, thought Frank, I need supervision here! It's all very well busking it with witnesses, but when an interview turns up a new development like this one, I am simply not experienced enough to know how to follow it up.

What the hell was wrong with the man, anyway? Had his dog got run over?

If Queer Gear noticed Frank's floundering, or Don's zombie state, she didn't show it. Instead, she continued enthusiastically, ''I expect everyone is telling you that they cannot possibly imagine why anyone should wish poor old Beans any harm, aren't they? Yes, I thought so. A polite fiction, I assure you, Constable. The sort of thing one is supposed to say under such circumstances. But the truth is, you know, we all have motives for killing him.''

''You have?'' said Frank, wondering what he was meant to do if this turned out to be a confession. ''For instance?''

''Oh, well, I was speaking generally, you know,'' she said. ''But if you want specifics, well…let us see… To whom have you spoken so far?''

He couldn't see any harm in telling her that. Didn't mean there wasn't any harm in it, but he couldn't see any. ''To Dill,'' he replied.

"The herb woman." Queer Gear nodded.

"And to the young man known as Weed."

"Ah yes, the hippy."

"Punk," said Frank.

"I beg your pardon?"

"He's got short hair. Can't be a hippy with short hair." Frank spoke with the authority of one who has watched entire series of pop-enlivened social history shows on BBC2.

"I don't think that matters these days, actually, Constable. The rules of entry to hippiedom have been relaxed considerably in recent years, I fear, along with so much else. But he's definitely not a punk: no safety pins, no spitting. And besides, his hair may be short, but it isn't actually shaven, is it?"

"No, no," said Frank, "shaven heads, that's skinheads, not punks."

"Well," said Queer Gear, with a smile that said she knew she was right but that she didn't intend to fall out over it, "whatever he is, purely as an exercise I'm sure I can supply you with credible motives for those two plotters, right off the top of my head."

"Please do." Frank realised now that what he should have said a moment earlier was that if hippies didn't have to have long hair any more, then punks didn't have to have safety pins. No way of working that into the conversation now without causing offence, though.

"Right you are." She steepled her fingers, and bobbed her chin up and down on their point. "Dill, first—now there was certainly a degree of rivalry between her and Beans over which direction the campaign against the land deal should take. You've heard about this proposed development of the site, I suppose?''

"We have," said Frank. ''Though it's hard to believe that a struggle for the leadership of an allotment society could end in murder.''

"Oh I don't know—stranger things have happened.''

"And Weed? Was he another frustrated candidate for the Chairmanship?''

"No, indeed! No...now, then, Weed...well, I did get the impression that Beans did not altogether approve of some of the crops which that young man was rumoured to grow on his allotment.''

"Is that right?'' Frank's antennae twitched at the hint of drugs. That was more like it—a proper, respectable, time-honoured motive for homicide.

Queer Gear blushed. ''But I think I have said too much there, Constable. I am only playing silly games, you understand, to put off the moment when you will leave me alone and I shall be forced to return to my word processor.''

An elegantly phrased invitation to bring the interview to an end, thought Frank. If only DI Packham had been fully *compos mentis*, though. Frank was sure this business of Weed's allegedly unorthodox cultivation was worth pursuing with the woman, perhaps even to the point of insistence, but he just wasn't sure how to do it without alienating her altogether.

Best leave it, he decided. We can always come back, when Don returns from his mental away-day.

The next problem was going to be getting Don out of the house and back into the car. Would he have to carry him there, fireman-style? And if so, what excuse would he make to the witness? *You'll have to forgive the Inspector. He's put his back out and he's too proud to take sick leave.*

In the event, however, and much to Frank's relief, Don got to his feet as soon as Frank got to his, like a bored but dutiful Labrador, and walked straight past Frank and the woman, opened her front door himself, and headed for the motor.

Evidently, thought Frank, he's left his manners wherever he left his tongue this morning.

As he and Queer Gear shook hands in the doorway, she looked over his shoulder to where Don sat in the passenger seat of the car, and said, "It's a pity cannabis is illegal. I've heard it can be most efficacious in such cases."

She spoke with such obvious sincerity that for a moment Frank forgot to be astonished by the content of her remark. And when he did hear it properly, on mental replay, he still wasn't sure what she meant. So he just said, "Thanks for your help," and left.

"I DON'T KNOW what was wrong with the old sod," he told his wife later. "I couldn't get a word out of him all day. Well, I say all day—he bloody disappeared in the afternoon. We only did the one interview, in the end."

"Disappeared?"

"We got back in the car, right, after the first interview of the day. And I say to him, like, Where to next, Guv? And he comes back with, Ah hell, let's call it a day."

"Great," said Debbie, swinging her legs up on to the sofa. "I could get used to CID hours."

"Yeah, but I'm not CID, am I? What if my sergeant finds out I've been skiving at home all afternoon?" He took a swig of tea, found it was cold, and set it aside.

"I don't call painting the spare bedroom skiving," said Debbie. She retrieved his mug, and finished his tea. She liked it cold.

"I'm not sure the skipper's very big on home maintenance, love. Not on company time, any rate."

"Well, you were only following orders, *Ja, Mein Herr?*" She could see he was really disturbed by all this. Not only because he was talking about work, which was uncharacteristic enough on its own, but more significantly because she'd hardly had a smile off him since he came through the door. And one of the reasons she'd chosen him was because he seemed incapable of removing the soppy grin from his chops for more than seconds at a time whenever he was in her company. Ah well—all marriages got old eventually, she supposed.

"If you could call them orders," Frank grunted. "What he actually said, his exact words were: 'What's the point, eh? I mean, we've all got to die some time, eh? I mean what does the death of one old geezer really matter in the great scheme of things, eh?'"

"I see what you mean," said Debbie, getting up to switch the telly on. She hoped there'd be some sport— any sport—on one of the channels, to distract him. "Not exactly a quotation from the rules and regs, was it?"

"I don't know." Frank shook his head in a transparently obvious externalisation of his desire to put the day behind him. "Maybe I should change my aftershave."

SIX

WHEN HE ARRIVED AT the nick the next day, Frank found no Don—and this time, no message from Don, either.

He changed out of his uniform, and decided there was nothing else for it; he'd have to brave the CID room.

There were three detectives in the open-plan office when he poked his head round the door—two men and a woman. He didn't know any of them as more than names, and wasn't sure how to elicit from these notoriously sarky, plod-despising egoists the information he required. *Excuse me, but has anybody handed in a DI?* was definitely out.

"You looking for Don Packham?" one of the female detectives called out, when she spotted him. She sounded friendly enough, so Frank advanced into the den and smiled at her.

"I am, yes. I think I'm supposed to be working with him today. No idea where he might be, I suppose?"

The look he received in reply—no words, just a look—could best be described, he reckoned, as "knowing." Which was all very well, but unfortunately, whatever it was she and her colleagues knew, nobody bothered to tell Frank Mitchell.

"Done a disappearing, has he?" said the elder of the two men, a plump, balding detective sergeant.

"I don't know, Sarge," said Frank. "I've had a quick look round the station, he doesn't seem to be—"

"Best place to look for DI Packham," said the woman, "is generally wherever you left him. Tried there, have you?"

If you all despise him so much, how come he's a DI and you lot aren't, was the question that came to Frank's mind. The words that came out of his mouth, however, were less confrontational. "Maybe he's overslept or something. Perhaps I should give him a ring?"

The detective sergeant pointed towards a phone on one of the unoccupied desks. "Go ahead. His home number's in the blue book there."

Uncomfortably aware of his small but attentive audience, Frank dialled the number and waited. After seven rings, he realised it wasn't going to be answered. After fifteen, he publicly admitted the fact.

"No reply," he said, to the room in general. The staff address book was still open at P, next to his elbow. He memorised the address listed for Don Packham, without, he hoped, appearing to do so. "He's probably on his way to the scene. I'll catch him there." A snort—male, he thought—came from somewhere off to his left. "Thanks for your help, anyway."

Don's car wasn't in the parking bay; Don wasn't in the nick; Don's phone didn't answer. And yesterday, Don had been about as lively as a kipper on a fishmonger's slab.

Jesus...what if he's...?

Frank got back into his own car, winkled the A-Z

out of the glove compartment, and drove as fast as he dared to West Hampstead.

The address given for Don Packham turned out to be a first-floor, walk-up flat in an old conversion, roughly equidistant between a pub and a Tube station. It was a quiet road, thought Frank, if you didn't count the noise.

The street door was unlocked, so Frank ascended to the first landing, where he stood for a moment outside Don's door, pondering on the delicate subject of knocking procedure.

What exactly was the etiquette here? If he hammered hard enough to rouse the dead, or even the dead drunk, and the DI opened up, live and well but wondering why the hell someone he hardly knew was trying to beat a hole in his door with bare hands, Frank'd look a bit of a Charlie, wouldn't he?

On the other hand, if he knocked quietly, politely, timidly—and all the while, the man was lying in there in a pool of his own vomit…or worse…

Pity there was no buzzer. Buzzer would have been easier to sort out.

Stop pissing about! he told himself. He took a deep breath, and gave the door three, four, five good, solid, copper's knocks. The usual result of which, in his experience, was that every other door in the place burst open, while the one you were standing outside remained inviolate, its occupant clambering out of the window with his socks in one hand and his share of the loot in the other.

In this instance, however, no other tenants appeared—but Don Packham did, after the third fusillade, wearing an oriental-print dressing gown that very obviously had been designed for a person of an altogether different gender. The DI also wore a sheen of bluish stubble, and, perched on his nose like a pair of broken specs, a clearly visible headache.

"Sir!" said Frank, relieved to see his boss still alive, and embarrassed to see him without his professional skin on. "I was just—er—"

"Frank? Jesus, man, what time is it?" The voice was rough, in keeping with the face, but neither accusatory nor, it seemed to Frank, noticeably depressed.

"Just before ten, sir. I wasn't sure what you wanted me to—"

"Just before ten? Oh God! Come in, mate, come in—you put the kettle on, I'll put some trousers on. Better yet, you put the kettle on, I'll have a shower."

The room Frank now entered—and which, it being empty of Don, he had a chance to take in in some detail—was about twice the size of his and Debbie's main bedroom. Against one wall, under a window looking out on to the street, was a double bed. At the other end of the room stood a coffee table, a TV on a stand, a sofa and two very battered armchairs, all grouped around a small gas fire. Between the two ends of the bedsit (or studio flat; wasn't that what they called them in London?) was a door, presumably to the bathroom, and a basic kitchenette: cooker, sink, fridge.

Lots of books and records, as Frank would have predicted, lay in piles here and there, some on shelves, some in cardboard boxes; but other than that there was little to say that an intelligent, professional man of middle years lived here. It could have been a room in a rather run-down hotel, Frank thought.

The kettle was boiling as Don reappeared, his hair wet, his chin still stubbled, his body clothed in suit trousers, unbelted, and blue shirt, unbuttoned. He wore nothing on his feet.

"Tea or coffee, sir?"

"Don, not 'Sir,'" said Don. "Don't worry, Frank, I'll take over that now I'm here. Big pot of tea, yeah? That do the job?"

"Sounds fine, Don, thanks."

"Yeah," said Don, on a long, enthusiastic, espresso hiss. "Big, hard bastard of a pot of tea. A three-bagger, black as Nero's heart, hot as Delilah's thighs and strong as Zeus. You take sugar, Frank? I bloody hope not, because I'm 99 percent sure there isn't any."

"I don't, in fact, no." He keeps calling me Frank, thought Frank; perhaps to be sure he remembers it. "Just a spot of milk, if you've got it."

Don pulled the fridge open with his right hand, while pouring boiling water into the teapot with his left. "Nope. Sorry, no milk."

"As it comes'll be fine, sir."

"Good. Just let that sit for a while, while I get the grub going. Let's see what we have got in this fridge… Bloody glad to see you on the doorstep this morning, Frank. Thanks a lot for coming over, I appreciate it."

"No problem—Don."

"Good man," said Don, his voice muffled by the fridge, which currently contained his head, a rummaging arm and at least one shoulder. "I overslept is what happened, Frank. A thousand apologies, pal—for putting you to this trouble." He backed out of the fridge, clutching clingwrapped and Tupperwared trophies.

"No matter." Frank just managed to stop himself from adding the patently absurd lie *I was in the area anyway.*

From on top of the oven hood, Don took the largest frying pan Frank had ever seen in private ownership, and banged it down on a hob. He started opening cupboard doors, seemingly at random. "Bloody stupid twat," he said. "I was drinking wine last night. Don't know why I do it, Frank—I'm a beer drinker, always have been. Wine always buggers me up."

"Uh-huh," said Frank, nothing else appropriate having entered his head.

"Yeah! Never would have woken up if you hadn't come knock-knock-knockin'. So, many thanks for that. And while we're at it," he said, breaking half a dozen eggs into the giant's pan, "many thanks, too, for all your excellent work so far on this case. I'm very impressed, Frank, truly I am, and I shall be saying as much to your inspector next time we bump into each other down the Freemason's."

Frank's jerked eyebrows produced an impish grin from Don. "That's a pub in Hampstead, Frank, in case you were wondering. Sorry, shouldn't take the woss-name, should I? Not after you've just saved my career, if not my life."

At this point, the DI suddenly remembered the tea, which was still brewing in its pot. Frank didn't reckon he'd seen tea made in an actual teapot since he'd left his mum's, and when he tasted this stuff he thought he could maybe guess why.

"That strong enough for you, Frank? I know you northern men can't stand anything sweet and milky, right?"

"Right, yeah," said Frank; but then he had to say it again, because the first time, he had still been adjusting to life without a throat, rendering him inaudible to all but dogs and spiritualists.

"Fascinating business, this allotment murder, don't you reckon?" said Don, slicing mushrooms and garlic. "A real puzzle, dead meaty."

Frank wasn't sure whether "dead meaty" was a pun or merely an unfortunate turn of phrase. Either way, best ignored with the room now full of the smell of sizzling bacon. "It's certainly an interesting case, sir. Though, of course, I've not got much to compare it with, this being my first murder."

"Of course it is, I keep forgetting—you look the part so well. Here we are, then, breakfast is served."

"For me, sir?"

Don waggled two huge plates full of food. "Well Christ, man, you don't think I'm going to eat both of these myself do you? I like my grub, but I'm no hero!"

Frank couldn't imagine eating *one* of them on his own. The plates, built in proportion to the gargantuan frying pan, were so covered with food that none of the pattern was visible. In fact, now he came to think of it, it was only convention that made Frank suppose that these two-inch thick piles of fried food were, in fact, seated on crockery at all. For all he knew, they might be self-supporting, woven together by some sort of culinary origami.

"You *do* like fry-ups, do you?"

"Oh, indeed, sir, yes I do," said Frank, thinking *on lazy Sunday mornings, when I haven't got to do a day's work after, I do.* But he took one of the plates, hoping he'd chosen the smaller one, if such a thing existed, and added, "Ta very much, sir. Champion."

Almost dancing on the spot with enthusiastic anticipation, Don sat on the sofa and perched his plate on his knees. Frank followed suit. "There you go," said Don. "You can't beat that for a hangover cure: eggs, bacon, fried bread, mushrooms, tomatoes, garlic. Damn!" He stood up, and returned to the kitchen area. "Forgot the HP sauce. Or do you prefer Tabasco? And salt, pepper, mustard…"

Sounded like he was going to start skipping, thought Frank. Wouldn't put it past him, either; this is a different man to the zombie I was saddled with yesterday. If this is what having a hangover does for him, you wonder why he wants to cure it.

Have to admit though, he knows a thing or two about fry-ups. Frank hadn't tasted food like this since his brief, unglamorous bachelor days. He was sure Debbie would cook it for him if he asked, but—well, the fact was that this wasn't the kind of food people like him and Debbie ate. A moderately indulgent bank holiday bacon and eggs, maybe, but the full, greasy monty…for all that southerners thought everyone with a northern accent of any sort was automatically a member of the industrial proletariat, Frank knew better. Frank knew what he was, where he'd started, and where he aimed to finish. And one thing he knew for certain: middle-class folk do not eat fry-ups.

Christ, but it tasted bonny, but!

"Fucking good nosh, eh?" said Don, chuckling through a mouthful of the very food he was praising.

Looking up, Frank got the feeling that the DI had been keeping watch on his face, waiting for the tell-tale early signs of gastronomic rapture to appear there. He smiled, and nodded vigorously. "Yes indeed, sir—fucking excellent nosh!"

Don returned the smiles and nods, then swallowed his mouthful, looked down at his plate, and said, rather more thoughtfully, "All except the bacon, really."

"Why?" said Frank, who'd just that second stuffed half a rasher into his mouth. "What's wrong with the bacon?" He remembered Don exploring the fridge like a pot-holing palaeontologist. Visions of pre-war sell-by dates shimmered before him.

"No, nothing, nothing," said Don, quickly. "Sorry, didn't mean to give you a fright. No, don't worry, it's top class bacon this is, free range. All I meant was—well, I have to try and forget what it is I'm eating, if you know what I mean. You know—pigs. Beautiful creatures they are, they deserve a better fate than this."

Frank knew what he meant, though he had to search his memory; yes, he'd felt like that once, years ago. He supposed that all kids did; meat-eating did not come naturally to children, whatever folk said. But he'd had it—well, not beaten out of him, but, say, socialised out of him. And just as well, else there'd be a hell of a lot of unemployed butchers in the world, all running around the place leaving their cleavers between people's shoulderblades.

"You thinking of going vegetarian, sir?"

Don shook his head, gave his lips a rueful twist. "No, not seriously. Though we'll all have to sooner or later; this planet can't support cattle farming for much longer. But for the time being, I'll eat it as long as it's legal!" With fork and hand, he matched word to deed. "Mind you, I went out with a veggie girl once. Few years back. Ate nothing but vegetarian for three months, and I'll tell you what—I was never hungry. It's a surprisingly rich, varied cuisine, with thousands of years of history behind it, all over the world. And another thing…"

As Don continued his address on the pros and cons of the meat-free diet, Frank marvelled at his loquacity. It was as if he were making up for lost time, talking twice as much today to fill in the blanks of yesterday. Would he ever, in fact, stop?

As the DI paused to take a swig of tea, Frank asked, "You've never been married then, sir?"

"You ask me a question like that," Don began, and Frank cringed: *Oh Christ, I've gone too far!* "You ask me a question like that," Don repeated, "and you call me Don. OK? Because let's face it, Frank, it is abso-fucking-lutely ridiculous to ask a bloke a question as personal as that, and then stick Sir on the end of it. Isn't it?"

"Yes, sir," said Frank, very deliberately. "Abso-fucking-lutely."

"Right. So I don't want to have to tell you again." Don put his empty plate on the floor beside his chair, and lit one of his small cigars. Funny, Frank thought, he wasn't smoking yesterday. Perhaps that's why he was so miserable, because he was trying to give up.

"Married?" said Don, through a smoke ring. "No, not entirely. Lived with a few women, off and on, now and then. Never for more than a few months at a time as it's turned out. I'm probably not the marrying kind, truth be told. But how about you? You're married?"

"Yes." Just as Frank didn't like talking about work

at home, so he preferred not to talk about home at work. But he'd walked into this, hadn't he?

"Kids?" asked Don.

"One on the way. Due in August."

"Excellent," said Don, smiling like an uncle. "I envy you that—bet you can't wait, eh?"

"Right," said Frank, and there followed a slight silence, until Don apparently got the message.

"So, from what we've learned so far, what do you reckon? Arthur Beans Jones was killed by one of his ten allotment neighbours, right?"

"Looks like it," agreed Frank, noting that the DI had apparently heard what was said yesterday, even if he hadn't been listening.

"In which case," Don continued, "was it a spur of the moment thing?"

"I would say so, yes," said Frank. "I mean, given where and how the body was found—if you were planning the perfect crime, you'd surely come up with something better than that. Even given that the actual spot of the killing was pretty sheltered, it's still got to be a very risky time and place to kill someone."

"That's true." Don's cigar waggled between his lips as he spoke. "On the other hand, the facts also fit a hypothesis of premeditated murder, if you allow that the killer might have been interrupted by some unexpected development. Some-one coming over to Beans's plot to borrow a spade, for instance."

"That is true," admitted Frank. "And if we're following that line, then I suppose a bean trench isn't a bad place to dump a body."

"How so?"

"In order to delay discovery, I mean. Maybe the

killer was interrupted, or feared he or she was about to be interrupted, but had intended to fill in the trench on top of the body, giving him time to establish an alibi.''

"Good point," said Don. "Yes, and now I think about it, there was a load of soil mounded around the trench, wasn't there?''

"That's how you do bean trenches, yes. Take out the soil, fill the trench with compostable material, then refill with the excavated earth.''

"How long would that take?" asked Don. "You being our resident Percy Thrower.''

Frank thought about the question. If he was going to earn respect from a senior detective for his expertise in allotment matters, then he'd better live up to it. After all, any "in" with CID was better than none. "If you were a fit person, used to that sort of work, then I daresay you could fill in a trench that size in, say, fifteen minutes? Maybe less. Working flat out, like.''

"So," said Don, eyes half-closed. "You go over to Beans's plot, picking a moment when you're fairly sure nobody's looking your way. You get him in conversation, and move him over to the trench on some pretext—'Oh Mr. Beans, please show me how you make your wonderful bean trenches!'—you knock him into the trench, grab his fork and shove it through him. Then remove the fork, backfill the trench, and scarper. I guess you could reasonably expect to perform a routine like that in twenty minutes, with the wind behind you. You agree?''

"If all went according to plan, yes," said Frank. "And if all didn't go according to plan—as in this case—then provided nobody sees you going onto or leaving the allotment, you're still no worse off, in terms of being a suspect, than any of the others.''

''OK, then. So we have half-way decent scenarios for both murder and manslaughter—in the latter case, obviously, some sort of argument that got out of hand. Do we also have a half-way decent motive?''

''From the three we've seen so far, you mean?''

''Stick with them, for now, yes.''

''Well, there's the hippie—Weed. If he is actually growing cannabis on that plot, then there could be an amount of money involved.''

Don shook his head. ''Not keen on that, Frank, not really. OK, what you say is true as far as it goes, but only if Weed is dealing, and if he is, I've never heard of him. Besides, could you really grow enough on a patch of ground that size, out in the open like that, to turn a decent profit? I wouldn't have thought so. We both know that home-grown tends to be for home consumption. Another thing. You'd be running the risk of someone recognising your crop, and turning you in. It's a pretty distinctive plant, if I remember correctly from my younger days.''

Frank assumed he meant his younger days in the Force, but didn't care to pursue the question; he knew Don had joined the Job comparatively late in life. ''I suppose if someone did get suspicious, you could always claim it was a green manure of some kind.''

''A green what?'' Don sputtered. ''No, on second thoughts don't tell me, not so soon after breakfast. Sounds disgusting!''

''We'll forget Weed for the moment, then, shall we?'' said Frank, not wanting to get identified in the

DI's mind with a cul-de-sac line of inquiry. "How about the American woman, Dill?" They were both using the plot names in preference to the suspects' given ones, Frank noticed; a lot easier to learn than a bunch of Johns and Marys—just as long as they boned up on the others in time for court.

"Dill?" said Don. "There was certainly tension between her and Beans over this development scheme, wouldn't you say? Could be that her bid for leadership of the Plotters Liberation Army necessitated removing the incumbent."

"In which case, we're back looking at an unplanned crime, presumably. An argument turning physical, or even an accident followed by panic."

"Why so sure, Frank?"

"Well, because—I mean, you'd hardly *plan* to kill someone over something so trivial, would you?"

Don pursed his lips. "Maybe, maybe not. You never know in this game, Frank. Remind me to bore you with my theory about that sometime."

"Which leaves, so far, the lady novelist, Queer Gear. She's pretty keen on murder mysteries—writing them as well as reading them. But I don't really suppose she could be researching her next book by killing folk, do you?"

"No," Don agreed, "you'd have to be a complete nutter for that, wouldn't you? And she didn't strike me as crazy. Rather misanthropic, perhaps, but not mad."

Frank had found her more charming than misanthropic, and wondered what she'd done to get up the DI's nose. Just caught him on the wrong day, perhaps?

"And assuming she's not mad," he said, "I can't think of any sensible motive for her. Yet, anyway."

"Agreed," said Don. "But it's early days. We shall press on, and employ the dialectic."

"Sir?"

"It means talk to people, Frank," Don explained with a not entirely reassuring wink. Christ, thought Frank, he's not a bloody Marxist, is he?

"Right. So who do we do next? You got the lists there, Frank?"

Frank passed over the two lists of plotholders, and after a few moments' scrutiny, Don said, "This solicitor bloke. We don't know his plot name, but elsewhere he goes by Jeremy Morgan. We'll have a go at him first, I reckon. They're not allowed to gossip at work, are they, so with a bit of luck he'll be full of pent up chit chat if we can winkle him out of his office."

THE WINKLING OF Jeremy Morgan did not prove difficult; he seemed only too happy to join the two policemen for an early lunch at a wine bar near his office in the centre of Harrow. Probably because he reckons we'll be paying, thought Don, who held a traditional copper's view of solicitors.

His diagnosis of the lawyer's mercenary motives was not undermined by the fact that Mr. Morgan chose a seafood salad from the menu (his companions stuck to liquid refreshment), but a mineral water from the wine list.

As Morgan excused himself to "wash his hands," Don whispered: "My mistake, Frank—this one knows how to keep his lips tight, on or off duty." He took

Weed's list of aliases from his jacket pocket, studied it briefly, and then showed it to Frank. "What's the betting?" he said, pointing at one of the nicknames.

Frank smiled. "That'll be him, I'd put money on it."

"So you don't like him either?" laughed Don. "Well, here he is, we'll ask him, shall we?"

As the lawyer resumed his seat, Don said, "Hands nice and clean now, sir? I understand they call you Mr. Perfect down on the allotments?"

"I'm afraid I don't know what you're talking about, Detective Inspector," Morgan replied, his face flushing slightly. He was a prosperous looking man—prosperous but boneless, recognisable as a solicitor from thirty yards.

"Oh you know, Mr. Morgan," said Don, with a matey grin—and you bloody do know as well, he thought. I'd lay money on that. "The nicknames all you happy plotters have for each other. There's Mr. Perfect, and Weed and a lady known as Queer Gear."

"And Beans," Frank put in. "Don't forget Beans, sir—the deceased."

Mr. Perfect—Don really had no doubt whatsoever that this was Mr. Perfect, in the flesh—declined, with a slight, fly-shooing shake of his head, to comment further on the matter of the alleged nicknames, so Don let it drop. He had seen that look many times before: the look of a solicitor who knows that you know he's not telling the truth, and also knows that there is no reason on earth why he should give a damn that you know.

"Have you had the allotment long, Mr. Morgan?"

"About eight months," Mr. Perfect replied. "I have

a young family, you see, and my wife and I became concerned about the safety of our food. All these health scares, you know—pesticides, food poisoning…''

''Oh I know,'' said Don emphatically. ''Enough to put you off eating anything you haven't grown yourself, isn't it? You'd be what they call an organic gardener, then, I take it?''

Mr. Perfect's upper lip twitched, briefly, in what was unmistakably a tic of distaste. ''Hardly, Detective Inspector. One does not need to join the Save The Rain Forests brigade simply in order to grow the odd bunch of carrots.''

''No, of course,'' said Don, his empathy still in place. ''Quite so. But you and your lady wife get on well enough with the others there, I imagine? A decent enough lot, you'd say?''

For some reason, this question seemed to involve more pre-response thinking time than had its predecessors. At last, the lawyer said, ''My wife rarely accompanies me to the allotment; it's not her sort of thing at all. And as for myself, I don't mix overmuch with the other tenants. I am there to grow food, not to gossip. Which is more than one could say for some of them.''

''You'll not have attended the action group meetings then?'' said Don.

Again, there seemed to be some careful consideration going on behind Mr. Perfect's silver spectacles before he answered. ''If you refer to the Allotment Society Extraordinary Meetings,'' he said, pronouncing each capital initial, ''then the answer is yes, I have attended.''

"These would be the meetings about resisting the bulldozers, right?"

"Concerning the proposed developments, Detective Inspector, yes. I had thought that a legal training might prove of some value at these gatherings, pathetic affairs that they were."

"And do you suppose," said Don, "that this development scheme might provide a motive for Mr. Jones's sad death?"

Mr. Perfect snorted. How do they do that without anything coming out, Don wondered.

"I very much doubt that, Detective Inspector. Very much doubt that. I wouldn't wish to tell you your business, of course, but I am quite sure that when you look you will find a sexual motive lurking at the bottom of this matter." He blatantly enjoyed their looks of surprise for a moment before adding, "Oh yes, gentlemen, in my profession one soon realises that man's bestial side never leaves him, no matter what age he might achieve."

That seemed to Don to call for a moment's gobsmacked silence, and he allowed one to pass, before saying, in a more serious tone, "You do realise, Mr. Morgan, that because of the peculiar circumstances of the death, all ten of you who rent allotments at that end of the site, not forgetting husbands, wives and servants, and who were all present on the site on Sunday morning, are, for want of a better term, suspects; and furthermore, that none of you has what might reasonably be called an alibi?"

"I really don't think I need an alibi, Detective Inspector, since there cannot be by definition anything linking me to the crime. I have no motive; I had no involvement.''

"Fair enough. And putting aside sex for the moment, if we may, you have no suggestions as to what sort of motive any of your fellow allotmenteers might have harboured?''

Mr. Perfect dabbed at his mouth with a paper handkerchief, though he'd long ago finished eating. Don recognised the subtitles—I'm a busy man, I've got to be going. "All I can tell you,'' said the lawyer, "is that these gardening types take their gardening very seriously. They can get very competitive about it all.''

"Did Arthur Jones enter competitions, do you happen to know?''

"That wasn't quite what I meant, Mr. Packham, but, as a matter of fact, yes, I believe he did—his runner beans, you know. Ghastly, great stringy things.'' Mr. Perfect found time in his busy schedule for a well-bred shudder.

"Any other competition fans on the site?'' Don asked.

"Hmm? Oh I don't know—I think that writer woman—''

"Daphne Lender?''

"I think she enters the local show occasionally, with her weird monstrosities.'' An offended frown broke the tan on Mr. Perfect's forehead. "She's quite a well-respected novelist, you know—I even saw her on an arts programme on BBC2 once. Hardly the sort of person one expects to find digging on an allotment site!''

WHEN THE LAWYER had left, Don decided it was time for lunch.

"We only just had breakfast,'' Frank gasped.

"I know," said Don. "I always find eating gives me an appetite, don't you?"

Frank's digestive system urged him to head disaster off at the pass with a quick change of subject. "What I don't get, Don, is why Mr. Perfect hires an allotment when he obviously despises the whole business?"

"Odd isn't it?" Don murmured, most of his attention focused on the menu.

"I suppose," Frank continued, "the answer could be the obvious one—he needs somewhere to get away from the missus." From childhood days on his granddad's plot, he recalled this being a not uncommon motive for persistent horticulture.

"Could be," said Don, looking up, but marking his place on the menu with a finger. "But what's wrong with the golf club? Or the Rotarians? Or good old-fashioned working late at the office?"

"Yeah...interesting, don't you reckon?" Don's response was a grunt, so Frank pressed on. "So, all that stuff about produce competitions—you don't really reckon that for a murder motive, do you?"

"No less likely than Mr. Perfect's love triangle theory, Frank. And even on that, we need to keep an open mind."

"I suppose you're right, yes. What about Mr. Perfect himself? Any motive there?"

Don set the menu to one side—mission accomplished or abandoned, Frank wondered. "His motive?" Don scratched his chin. "How about he thought poor old Beans made the place look untidy?" He signalled the waitress, who signalled back: *Only one pair of hands, mate.*

"You checked the suspects for previous yet, Frank?"

"Ah—not quite yet, sir," Frank replied. "There was some problem with the computer last night, and then this morning…" This morning I was in too much of a hurry, rushing to batter your door down to save you from your suicide bid. "This morning," he finished, "I forgot. Sorry."

"No problem, Frank. You'll just have to go and do it now. I'm afraid that means you'll miss lunch, mind. Pity, this selection of pates looks rather interesting, and as for the—"

"No problem," said Frank, leaping to his feet. "Enjoy your meal, Don."

When he returned to the wine bar forty minutes later, Don showed all the signs of having followed his advice, and was now completing his enjoyment with coffee and a cigar.

"Three of the ten are known to us," said Frank without preamble. "Weed, one count of possession, cannabis resin."

"Doesn't sound like the record of a drug baron."

"Not really," agreed Frank. "Unless he's been very careful or very lucky. Or just starting out?"

"Possible, I suppose. And who are the other two, or do I have to guess?"

"Dill—the American woman—for trading without a license."

"Trading without?" said Don. "Well, well. Any idea where?"

"Yes sir, I phoned the nick where she was arrested, managed to speak to the arresting officer. He recalled her quite well because she was, quote, such a loud-mouthed, stuck-up Yankee bitch-dog, unquote.''

"Really?" Don looked genuinely surprised. "I thought she was quite sweet, didn't you, Frank?''

"Sweet or not, she's been done four times in the last fourteen months for setting up a stall on the fringes of various North London street markets, selling herbal beauty preparations. Shopped by the other stall-holders, presumably.''

"You can bet on it," said Don. "They don't like space invaders, don't the market folk. But four times, eh? All cautions, or did she get prosecuted?''

"Paid a fine on the last occasion, which was more than six months ago. Nothing since, so either she learned her lesson or she's found a better outlet.''

"Got the message and applied for a license?" guessed Don.

"No, she hasn't," said Frank. "I checked.''

"Well done." Don gave him a comradely punch on the shoulder. "Good thinking. So, not sure how all that helps us with a murder inquiry, but it certainly gives us a different slant on Ms. Daniels, doesn't it?''

Frank had to think for a second or two before his brain made the connection between Ms. Daniels and Dill. "Oh yes," he said. "And the third one's even more interesting, I reckon.''

"Ah!" Don stubbed out his cigar, and leant forward. "The meat course! Go on, then.''

"Mr. Rodney Gorringe," Frank read from his notes, as if announcing arrivals at the Hunt Ball. "Management consultant, sixty-two years old at the time. Cautioned for kerb-crawling, two years ago.''

"Well," said Don on a long breath. "Kerb-crawling—still a sin that dares not speak its name in polite suburban company, wouldn't you say? Still, don't you think, a fit subject for blackmail?"

SEVEN

"YOU'LL FIND HIM—should you really wish to do so—upon his allotment." Mrs. Gorringe, who had answered the door at the archaically modernistic bungalow five minutes from the allotment site, was a starkly unattractive woman. No, thought Don: anti-attractive, that was more like it. And he suddenly smiled as the thought struck him that the word "repellent" meant much the same in colloquial speech as it did to physicists. At any rate, Don didn't blame her husband for his little hobbies, with a wife like this to drive him from his home. All spiky angles, she was, with one of those faces, so common in the more affluent suburbs, which suggested that their wearers were always ready to hate first, ask questions later.

"Likes his gardening does he, Mrs. Gorringe? That's good. Bit of exercise keeps a fellow young and virile, isn't that what they say?"

He heard Frank cough—in warning or embarrassment he couldn't be sure—behind him. Mrs. Gorringe contented herself with closing the door.

As they passed through the site gates, Frank recognised the squat, ruddy-faced figure of Mr. Gorringe—the man who'd tried to tell him his job when he and PC Standfield first got to the scene—energetically digging on an allotment to the right of the main path, and just past the invisible boundary between Tap End and Gate End.

"Your wife said we'd find you here, Mr. Gorringe," said Don. "Permission to come aboard?"

Gorringe waved them onto his plot. "I bet she did!" he said. "Well, I've got a lot of catching up to do, what with your lot having had the place sealed off for the best part of two days."

"Sorry about that," said Don. "Unavoidable, I'm afraid."

"Of course, of course, I'm not complaining. Could have been much worse. But you get nervous, you see, leaving the land alone, even for that short time. It's a good piece of land this, but it still needs management."

Frank mentally checked the list of nicknames, and quickly came up with what he was quite certain was the correct answer: The Squire. Yes, look at the way the old boy cradles his spade in his arm, as if it were a broken shotgun; look at the way he sniffs the air, gazing into the far distance of a horizon that was all of twenty yards away. The Squire, managing his land!

"Can't offer you tea or anything, I'm afraid," the Squire apologised, proudly. "Because I don't have the facilities. No shed on this plot, you'll notice, not like some of the others. Wanted to stay in a shed all day I could stop in the garden. I like to get out in the fresh air, me."

"Is that why you took up the allotment?" asked Don. "For the fresh air?"

The Squire nodded. "Took early retirement. Needed to do something to get me out of the house, bit of gentle exercise, and I was never one for golf—bloody stupid game—and jogging's even dafter. So here we are.'' He gestured about him at his imaginary acres of grouse moor. Frank suppressed a smile, and caught a wink from Don. ''Best decision I ever took—getting back to the land, that's what it's all about. Listen!'' he said suddenly. Don and Frank obediently struck harkening poses. ''Is that a cuckoo?''

Frank thought it was more likely a car alarm, but then he didn't pretend to be a countryman.

''How do you get on with the other plotholders?'' asked Don.

''Well, OK, nice enough bunch. Mind you, you can't tell them anything.''

''No?'' said Don.

The Squire shook his head. ''No! Take the chap next to me, for instance—Mr. Perfect they call him.''

''The solicitor?'' said Frank.

''Is he? Didn't know that, but it doesn't surprise me. Seems the type. Down here what a man does for a living is irrelevant; we're all brothers of the soil here. But when he took on that plot I told him, I said you won't have any luck there, mate.''

''Why's that?'' asked Don.

''Local contours. That plot floods in the spring, it's boggy all winter, and it dries up like concrete in the summer. He didn't take any notice, though.''

Don and Frank looked over at the next-door allotment, at its dark soil and neat rows. ''Seems to be doing all right, but,'' said Frank.

''Yes, well, he's had to buy in bloody cartloads of manure, though. Bloody cartloads.''

''Right,'' said Frank.

''Besides, the man has absolutely no interest in

country matters. Don't know why he doesn't just buy the stuff from the supermarket, save himself a lot of work.''

Since the police officers had been wondering the same thing themselves, they offered no comment to this. Instead, Don asked, ''You obviously have your ear to the soil around here, Mr. Gorringe. Any thoughts you'd like to share with us about this tragic business?''

''Looking for a murderer, right?'' The Squire stuck one hand in a pocket of his old tweed jacket. At least, it looked old; Frank wondered though if he hadn't bought it second-hand specially for the role. ''Well, not for me to point the finger, but you might like to try Compost Joe.'' He pointed his fork across the path. ''That's his plot there. Now it seems to me that whoever did for poor old Beans must have had more than just the one screw loose.''

''And that describes Compost Joe, does it?'' said Don.

''Put it this way, Superintendent. He grows nothing on his plot except compost. No crops, just heaps and heaps of bloody compost. Now if that's not crazy...''

''How about Beans, Mr. Gorringe?'' asked Don. ''You get on well with him? Was he an easy bloke to get on with?''

''Beans? Oh my God, splendid fellow! Marvellous fellow, I can't begin to understand how anyone could have had anything against him. Real old countryman, you know, full of the ways of nature. Could tell you anything about country lore.''

I bet he could, thought Frank. And you'd believe it, too.

. "Do you know," continued the Squire, putting a finger against Don's chest for added emphasis, "that man could tell you when it was going to rain, to within an hour. Marvellous man!"

Probably had a radio in his shed, thought Frank, who'd met plenty of amateur meteorologists growing up on Tyneside.

"Right," said Don. "Thanks for all that, there's just one thing more we'd like you to help us with, if you possibly could."

"Fire away," said the Squire, his round, red face almost splitting with self-importance.

"Tell us about the kerb crawling, Rodney."

Whatever effect the DI had hoped for from this cheekily throwaway question, Frank was willing to bet it wasn't the one he got.

With a bark of laughter, the Squire dropped his fork, and stuck his hands up above his head. "I surrender! You've got me bang to rights!"

"I see..." said Don, quite obviously searching his repertoire for a follow-up question.

"Well, really, what do you want me to say, Super-intendent?" said the Squire, still laughing, still holding his hands up, but with his face, Frank noticed, even redder than usual. "It was a long time ago, I was a naughty boy, got caught, got a ticking off, end of story. I mean, good Christ man, you've met my wife? Yes? Well, can you blame me?" He lowered his hands at last, and stuck them in his pockets. When he continued, he'd stopped laughing, and sounded altogether more sober. "Won't happen again, though, I can tell you that."

"Well," said Don, recovering, "that is the general idea of giving an offender a caution—"

"Caution? Fuck the caution, I don't give a shit about that, saving your presence. No, I'm talking about this place." He repeated his all-encompassing, landowner's sweep. "I've not been troubled by the old urges, not since I started on this lot. Stress of work, that's all that was. Once you've got your hands in the soil, well…you don't need all that stuff, believe me. You just don't need it."

"And does your wife take an equally sanguine view, sir?" said Don. "Oh, pardon me—she does know about the caution, I presume?"

The Squire wagged a naughty-naughty finger in Don's face. "Yes, my friend, the wife does indeed know all about it. Your lot sent a letter to my home address, didn't they? Standard practice, so I understand. Humiliate the punter. Grass him up to his wife and let her sort him out. Cheaper than taking the poor sod to court, eh? But you see, what they didn't know in my case was that the wife and I had not actually lived as man and wife, if you get my meaning, for many years. So she couldn't give a toss, pardon the expression, as long as it didn't get in the papers."

"So you weren't being blackmailed, then?" said Frank, though he was pretty sure what the answer would be. No man who publicly refers to his wife as "the wife" could have much shame, in Frank's view.

The Squire tipped his head back and laughed with his mouth wide open. An artificial gesture, but one which conveyed its intended message nonetheless. "Blackmailed? What an idea! No, no, fair enough question under the circs, I understand that, but listen:

when I first retired I used to do a bit of after-dinner speaking. That was before the allotment took over. On the management consultancy circuit, you know.''

''Sounds riveting,'' said Don.

''Well I don't know about riveting,'' said the Squire, unperturbed, ''but it always seemed to go down well enough. Better than the retired coppers on the circuit; they tend to amuse the drunks and offend everyone else.'' Big smile. ''Anyway, point is, that kerb crawling episode formed the basis for my star anecdote. I'm not kidding, I paid for a trip to Florida off the back of that incident.''

''So DOES THAT rule him out as a possible blackmail victim?'' said Frank, as they trudged back to the car.

''If he's telling the truth then, yes, I'd say so. Wouldn't you?''

''Yeah, I suppose so—if he's telling the truth.''

''We'll check,'' said Don. ''Here, you don't reckon old Beans could have been secretly servicing the lonely Mulch Widow, do you?''

''What? Mrs. Gorringe?''

''I know it's a pretty repugnant thought, Frank, but stranger things have happened. Probably. And it'd be a motive.''

Frank thought about it as they buckled their seat-belts. ''I'm not so sure it would be a motive, you know. I mean, would the Squire really give a monkey's who was seeing 'the wife' just so long as nobody pinched his dibber?''

Don had no idea what a dibber was, and laughed long and loud when Frank explained.

EIGHT

FOR THE SECOND MORNING running, Frank was enjoying the rare luxury of a leisurely breakfast. While he waited at home for the DI to ring him with the day's instructions, Debbie made him an Enthusiasm Omelette: "You put everything you've got into it."

"Everything except garlic, today," he'd told her. "Don't want to be had up for police brutality."

By nine he'd finished eating, and was beginning to get a bit edgy about the phone's reluctance to ring. Was this going to be a repeat of yesterday?

Reading his mind, Debbie said, "I like these CID hours. I could get used to this."

"Even when it means I don't get home until all hours?"

"You weren't too late last night," she said.

"No," he laughed. "But only because Don Packham suddenly took it into his head to drive down to bloody Wiltshire, to visit some old friend he hadn't seen in twenty years. Without telling the friend first, I might add. Let's hope the guy was at home. Or not, perhaps, for his sake."

"You're kidding!" She poured them both another cup of tea. "You know, I like the sound of your DI Packham. I mean, nobody could accuse him of being boring Mr. Middle Management, could they?"

"That's true," Frank agreed, giving the silent phone another accusing look. "But the thing is, what sort of mood's he going to be in this morning? Will he even be up to using the phone, or will I be sat here all day waiting for him to call, like a teenager getting stood up on a date? And what's my relief sergeant going to say when he sees my time sheets?"

"You blame it all on Don," said Debbie, with a shrug. "That's the great advantage of working for a hierarchical outfit; if your boss says it's all right, it's all right."

"I suppose so. But God, I hope he's in one of his good moods today. I'm not sure I can take too much more of the other sort."

"You know," said Debbie, thoughtfully, "it sounds a bit like manic depression."

"Well, who could blame me?"

"No not you, idiot!" She swiped him with a tea towel. "Your DI. Not clinical manic depression perhaps, though I don't really know a lot about that side of medicine. But mood swings, fantastic periods of manic energy followed by terrible slumps—"

"Followed by slumps," said Frank. "Exactly! Do you wonder I'm dreading hearing that phone ring almost as much as I'm dreading not hearing it?"

The phone rang.

Debbie watched anxiously as Frank listened, said "Yup" once or twice and "No" once. Eventually, unable to stand further suspense, she nudged his arm. He winked at her and used his free hand to deliver a thumbs up. Debbie mimed wiping sweat from a relieved brow.

FRANK PARKED HIS CAR behind Don's, in Crockett's Drive. Don got out of his own car and hopped into Frank's passenger seat.

"Good night last night, sir?" asked Frank, testing the waters. Mood swings meant what it said, didn't it? No law he knew of said that the mood had to last whole days at a time.

"Terrific, thanks, Frank. Bloody marvellous. Haven't seen this guy since we were demobbed from the Boer War, or somewhere round there, and we just picked up where we'd left off. As if one of us had popped out to the loo for five minutes, you know what I mean?"

"Sounds like a very jolly reunion," said Frank.

"That it was, boy, that it was. Tell you what, they've got some cracking beers down that way and all. I'd forgotten, I'm so used to drinking this London piss."

On that point, at least, both men could agree wholeheartedly. Both nodded, shook their heads, and sighed, as if drilled to do so by Busby Berkeley.

"Only got back to London an hour ago," said Don. "Haven't been to bed yet. Keep going, that's the best thing—you only get tired when you stop."

Or when you drop, thought Frank. "So, who's next on the list?"

"Joe Whiting."

"Ah," said Frank. "Compost Joe, I presume?"

"The same. He's here already; I checked when I arrived. So let's go."

Just before Dill's plot, and just across from the Squire's, there lay the mien of Compost Joe; and at labour upon it, its master—a short, slight man, with

Spam-top sandy hair and John Lennon specs, who was energetically pitchforking semi-rotted organic matter from a large, wooden container into a smaller, plastic one. Every now and then he paused to insert what appeared to be an eighteen-inch long thermometer into first one pile, then the other.

Close up, they could see that Joe's plot was covered almost entirely with compost heaps at various stages of disintegration, as well as containers of every imaginable sort, from wheelie bins (nicked from the local council, presumably) to elaborate bamboo cages, similar to those which once contained American POWs in Vietnam. It all reminded Frank of nothing so much as…well, of nothing really; he'd never seen anything like it.

Views of Compost Joe's empire from the paths were restricted—in order, Frank assumed, not to cause offence—by windbreak trellises. At the moment nothing grew on the trellises, but perhaps in summer, he thought, they would support nasturtiums or climbing beans.

Frank could detect the last remnants of a long-ago Mancunian accent, he reckoned, as Joe greeted them, plunging his pitchfork into the nearest heap, and wiping his hands on his overalls. "You looking for me, gents? If so, you're very welcome—I'm about due a breather."

Don made the introductions, and then gazed around him at Joe's plot, trying to think of something admiring to say about it.

Joe saw the look on his face, and interpreted it correctly. "Not exactly the Chelsea Flower Show, is it?"

he laughed. "But I like it, and it keeps me off the streets."

Behind the flippancy, Frank fancied he could hear an undertone of pride. He came from a long line of self-educated men, and he knew the sounds they made. Here was a man, if Frank was any judge, who would be more than happy to talk about his hobby. But then, what other kind of gardener was there?

"Do you not grow crops at all, Mr. Whiting?" he asked.

"Oh, Joe, please—call me Joe. If folk hear you calling me Mister, they'll think I've been nicked. Crops? No, not really, not much. Haven't got the time, tell you the truth." His laugh this time was just as wry, but perhaps a little less self-deprecating.

I was right, thought Frank; he takes this seriously. "So the obvious question, Joe," he said, his own laugh intended to defuse any potential offence, "is what do you do with all the compost you make?"

At that there was general laughter. "Bloody good question," said Don Packham. "If you can't come up with an answer, we might have to beat it out of you."

"Well, I give a lot of it away," said Joe, "same as everybody does with their surplus allotment produce, whether it's leeks or compost. And then, I do grow some crops. Spuds, mainly, as experimental subjects."

"What, you mean vivisection?" asked Don.

"To test the compost on, like. You know—which batch of compost gets the best results, and so on. I can see you two think I'm barmy. Thing is, I've always been interested in science, ever since school. I used to work as an assistant to a chemist in a research lab, then I got made redundant. So I started allotment gardening for something to do, you know, and for the cheap grub. But gradually I got more and more interested in composting. Especially winter composting techniques, most gardeners just give up as soon as the frosts start, and it's a terrible waste.''

"I know a lot of gardeners take composting pretty seriously, don't they?'' Frank remembered endless conversations on his granddad's site about secret recipes, magic mixtures, and something called night soil.

"Well,'' said Joe, unwrapping a Mars bar and biting into it with the air of a man who'd only had coffee for breakfast. Don Packham watched him eat it, with the air of a man who'd also only had coffee for breakfast. "You'll find a lot of plotters get interested in experimentation, become backyard scientists, so to speak. Not just those with formal scientific backgrounds. Like Dill, the American woman, and her herbal lotions.'' He frowned. "Mind, I'm not sure how much science goes into those. Still, she does look good for her age, doesn't she? What it is, you know, everyone's aware of the role of allotments in giving dispossessed peasants back their land. But until the industrial revolution forced specialisation on society, everyone was their own scientist. Their own doctor, their own naturalist, their own meteorologist…so this is just another aspect of using allotments to get back to your roots.''

"Fascinating,'' said Don, and showed every sign of meaning it. Though you could never tell with him, thought Frank; he was good at the old pokerface trick when he wanted to be.

Compost Joe obviously came to a similar conclusion, as he gave another short laugh, and said, "Anyway, you didn't come here to talk about compost did you? Except in the most roundabout way.''

"How's that?'' asked Frank, missing the reference.

"Trench composting,'' Joe explained. "Like what Beans died in—a compost trench. It's quite an interesting subject, actually, and surprisingly controversial. I hope to do some work on it myself if I ever get round to it.''

"What did you make of Beans?'' asked Don. "Get on with him all right?''

"He was a nice enough old chap,'' said Joe. "Bit quiet. Rather modern in his outlook.''

"Modern?'' said Frank.

"Sorry.'' Joe shook his head. "I meant, modern in the sense that he followed what are incorrectly called traditional gardening methods, rather than modern methods, which are of course, the real traditional ones.''

"Ah,'' said Frank, groping towards insight. "You mean he wasn't all that interested in compost?''

"Yeah!'' Joe pushed his specs back up his nose with a long finger. "I am an obsessed eccentric. I do not deny it. But it's a harmless enough obsession as these things go, wouldn't you say?''

"Is that how your fellow plotters view it, Joe?'' asked Don. "It doesn't offend them that your plot is all covered over with compost bins?''

Joe took his glasses off and started polishing them on a grubby handkerchief. "I don't think anybody's that bothered, to be honest. We all get on all right, pretty much. No, the only thing that worries me is if they reinstate plot inspections.''

"Who's that, the council?''

Joe nodded. "They used to do it, years ago, but then what with half the staff being laid off, it fell by the wayside. Now though, allotments are back in fashion—it goes in swings and roundabouts like everything else, what with health scares and so on—and plot take-up is much higher than it has been for a while. Two, three years ago about a third of this site was vacant."

"And you don't reckon your compost lab would pass muster?" said Don.

"Well, I'm not sure. It's no untidier than a lot of the standard, veg-and-two-flowers plots. But people might say it's unproductive—a waste of land." He picked up his fork, and began moving back towards his compost heaps. He wasn't being rude, Frank decided, he was just incapable of resisting the magnetic lure of rotting grass cuttings for very long. "Mind, if you ask me," Joe continued, "productivity isn't everything. I mean look at that bloke's plot over there—Mr. Perfect they call him. Plenty of crops, sure, very productive. But all in straight little lines, all uniform, all F1 hybrids. You can get stuff like that down the supermarket. What's the point? Daft sod bloody *buys* in his compost!" Joe shook his head in wonder, at what was clearly the strangest perversion he had ever encountered.

Frank looked questioningly at Don, who nodded. "Well thanks very much, Joe," Frank began. "We won't keep you any—"

"Course, you do realise he's one of them, don't you?" said Joe, his attention still with Mr. Perfect and his deficiencies.

"One of them?" said Don, turning back from the

path. Which them would this be, then—homosexuals? Catholics? Arsenal fans? People who use the wrong brand of weedkiller, and their best friends won't tell them?

"You do know who he is?" Joe drove the pitchfork back into the warmth of the heap.

"A solicitor?" Don guessed.

"Exactly." Joe put both his hands behind his back and shook hands with himself. Having done this, he brought one of the hands up to his face and laid a finger alongside his nose. He winked. "Exactly!"

"He means," said Don as they fought their way to the front of the lunchtime queue for bar meals at the nearest pub, "that Mr. Perfect is a Freemason."

"What, and that explains why he grows his veg in rows and doesn't make his own compost?" said Frank, still puzzled by Compost Joe's contorted mime.

"Maybe. They certainly have weird rules about most things, don't they, these Masonic loonies?"

"I wouldn't know, sir," said Frank, a little more stiffly than he had intended.

"Oh Christ, come on, Frank!" Don's face clouded. "Do you think I'd still be a bloody Detective Inspector if I knew the secret handshakes?"

And that was just about the last thing Don did say to Frank that day. Frank watched with growing despair as the DI changed his order from a pint of bitter to half a bottle of house red, sinking further into silence with every swig.

What the hell's brought this on? Frank wondered, before telling himself that whatever the cause was didn't really matter. The salient point was that Don was undeniably on the way down again, and there was no point in attempting to continue with the day's work.

Ah well—Debbie would be pleased to see him home early. Perhaps she was right: there were advantages to working CID hours.

NINE

FRANK LOOKED AT his watch for the tenth or eleventh time that morning: just past nine. He looked in his rear-view mirror: still no sign of the DI. He went back to rehearsing his lines.

Assuming Don was still in the state he'd been in when they'd parted last night, Frank was going to have to take the lead in this morning's interviews. And somehow he needed to establish that fact early on, without giving offence. All that, of course, was assuming Don turned up at all to the rendezvous outside Mrs. Rutter's house which they had arranged yesterday—or rather, which Frank had suggested, insistently, and several times, in the hope that it would lodge in Don's memory.

By nine fifteen, he was getting more than edgy, and wondering why the hell he hadn't arranged to meet at Don's place instead. No, he knew why, really: he couldn't face the thought of another massive breakfast (the last one had left him feeling dopey all day), and even more he couldn't bear the thought of knocking on Don's door and being told to bugger off.

Frank didn't know what to do. He was on the verge of ringing Debbie on his mobile to ask her advice, when a bang on the roof of his car made him leap so much he was lucky not to go through the windscreen.

The source of the bang took him a moment to comprehend, so entirely unexpected was it—not in its person, not even in its manner, but in its style.

"Morning!" said Don Packham, as Frank wound down the window. "Thought I had a spot of flu coming on last night, hence this—I always find physical exercise helps fight off infection, don't you?"

Frank looked at the crash helmet, the fluorescent jacket, the goggles, the face mask. "I didn't know you were a cyclist, Don," he said, judging that anyone who looked like that, and glowed like that, and spoke like that, and acted like that at that time of the morning was definitely Up and Don, not Down and Sir. "That looks like quite a serious machine."

"So they told me when I bought it, Frank, so they told me. Mind, I wouldn't really know. I've had it six months; this is the first time I've ridden it."

The DI disappeared from Frank's view peremptorily, and then reappeared without his bike. "I've chained it to your bumper," he explained. "So if either one of our vehicles gets nicked, at least we're in the same boat." He passed his helmet, goggles, windcheater, water bottle and sundry other items through the window to Frank. "Chuck these on your back seat, will you? I don't really fancy lugging them about for the rest of the morning."

As THEY WALKED UP the short path to Mary Rutter's front door, they could hardly fail to notice that this was not the Cowden of plush houses and neat bungalows. The Rutter's solid, whitewashed semi was self-evidently council or ex-council; and Don knew that, whatever the occupants might hope or believe, to a snob there would never be any difference between council and ex-council properties.

Even its location gave it away: set apart from the main thoroughfares of the suburb, amidst others of its kind, so as not to cause offence to the worthy mortgage payers as they scurried home from the Tube station each night.

Daft thing is, Don thought, I'd rather have this than any of the other places we've seen.

"Nice, isn't it?" said Frank, earning a warm nod of agreement from Don. Waiting for an answer to their ring on the doorbell, they looked around them at the lawn—mown but not clipped—the cheerful flower beds, the tricycle lying overturned on the grass. With the sun shining, the whole place gave off a welcoming air, from outside at least, of happy families.

Frank was just about to ring again, when the door was suddenly opened by a plump, blond woman in her early thirties, whose face carried a sheen of sweat. Healthy sweat, Don immediately diagnosed, the sweat of a busy mother, not the sweat of an invalid or a liar.

"Mrs. Rutter? I'm Detective Inspector Don Packham, this is Constable Frank Mitchell. Could you spare us a few moments?"

"You're here about poor old Beans," she replied, speaking through a gap between door and frame, which she was carefully guarding in that way unique to owners of small children and skittish pets. "Hold on a second, will you? I'm just going to shut the door again while I chain the toddler up."

A few minutes later, the two policemen sat in Mary Rutter's lived-in living room, drinking tea and trying not to allow her to persuade them to finish the packet of chocolate biscuits. As it turned out, she was better at persuasion than they were at resistance.

Child noises came from other parts of the house, as Mrs. Rutter glugged her tea as if it were the first liquid she'd taken in a week, and then lit an Embassy with a look of mixed gratitude and bliss.

"So, Mrs. Rutter—"

"Mother Hubbard," she interrupted, with a surprisingly shy, girlish giggle. "That's what they call me down the allotments."

"Ah," said Don. "I was wondering."

"Why Mother Hubbard?" asked Frank. "Wasn't she the one who went to the cupboard to—"

"Get her poor doggie a bone," said the woman. "Yeah, I know, and we haven't even got a dog. Tell you the truth, I think they were thinking of that old woman who lived in a shoe and had so many children she didn't know what to do. Because that's me, that is! But I believe it was that American woman, Dill they call her, who came up with most of the names, and she probably doesn't know our nursery rhymes, don't you reckon?"

"How many kids have you got?" asked Don.

"Five, and the oldest isn't yet ten." She raised her eyebrows and dropped her jaw, as if in disapproval of someone else's weaknesses. "Ridiculous, isn't it? But two of them are twins, and one of them was an accident." She laughed again, more boldly this time. "That's our excuse anyway, and we're sticking to it!"

"What does your husband do?"

"I should have thought that was obvious," she said, getting a chuckle from Don and a slight blush from

Frank. "No, he's with the Post Office. Does a lot of overtime, believe it or not."

"I'm surprised you've time for an allotment, with a big family," said Don. "Glutton for punishment, are you?"

"Must be," said Mother Hubbard. "No, well, originally it was just somewhere to go with the children. That can be a problem, you know, when you've got so many. Too expensive to take them all for a burger or whatever, even if you could get them all there without hiring a minibus!"

"So you thought the occasional day out amid the cabbages and peas might keep 'em quiet? Were you already a keen gardener?"

"No, not at all. Never had a garden before we moved here, and Les—my husband—just about mows the lawn and that's his lot. But I heard something on the radio about allotments and, you know, it seemed like a good way of stretching the pennies, getting healthy food for the kids and so on." She took a last drag on her cigarette, and stood up to refill her guests' teacups. "Mind, I'm dead keen on it now. Watch all the TV programmes, get the books out of the library, the whole business. Best thing I ever did, getting that allotment. But I bet you're bored with hearing that, aren't you? We're always saying that to each other, us plotholders!"

"Do you get on well with the others, then?"

"Oh they're a friendly enough crowd, for the most part. Up the Tap End, at least, don't have much to do with the other end."

"And Beans? Did you get on well with him?"

Her face fell, and she put her knuckles to her mouth.

"Oh he was a lovely old bloke, poor old chap. Very friendly."

"That's interesting," said Don, "because we've heard him described as being a bit, well, taciturn, perhaps?"

"No, I wouldn't say so. Not a great chatterbox, perhaps, could be a bit impatient I suppose. But very fond of the kids, always giving them little jobs to do on his plot, you know. Which was very kind, because it kept them from stopping me working!" She frowned, pushing her hair off her brow. "If some of the others found him a bit uncommunicative, perhaps they weren't always willing to make the effort. One or two of them, they could be, well, not stuck-up exactly, but you know…a bit superior, maybe. You know how people sometimes are with old folk? Whereas me, you see, I worked in an old folk's home before I married, so I got all that out of my system!"

"Sounds like you've lost a real friend there," said Don, softly.

"He was an old dear, he really was. There aren't many left like him. And he knew this area like the back of his spade, he really did. Nothing he couldn't tell you about local history and that. It was fascinating to hear him talk about the old days."

Don murmured, but he wasn't really listening to her testimonial. He was too busy thinking back over something she'd said a little earlier, and wondering how he might return to it without losing her trust.

After all, he had no actual reason to even consider the possibility that Beans had been a child molester. Except that…well, we're none of us immune to sensationalism. And, Christ, it does happen. And despite what the public likes to think, child molesters aren't always disfigured monsters. They're often nice old chaps (and chapesses, more often than anyone cares to admit) who just happen to be prey to unacceptable urges.

He'd have to be subtle. Trouble was, this woman was no idiot. "You say he was very fond of the kids. Now, did you ever—"

Her face went white, and her mouth narrowed. "Do you think I'm daft, or what? I do read the papers, you know. I do watch the cop shows on telly."

"Of course, Mrs. Rutter, it's just that—"

"I would never let my kids talk to anyone I wasn't sure about. Never! Well, would you? And I'd certainly never let them out of my sight, even with someone I was a hundred percent sure of. And old Beans, Inspector, him I *was* a hundred percent sure of. So would you have been if you'd known him."

Sure, thought Don; but if you had killed him because he'd been at your children, then that's exactly what you would say, isn't it?

Still, no point in pursuing it now. He liked this woman: liked her easy manner, liked her comfortable home. He envied her husband and her kids. And she was bright, too: more insight than any of the others they'd spoken to, no doubt about that. So he asked, straight out: "Who do you reckon did it, then? Knowing them all as you do, knowing Beans: who do you think killed him?"

The question seemed to shock her as much as his tentative probing about child abuse had. "None of that lot!" she gasped, from behind her hands. She shook her head. "No, couldn't be one of the plotters. No way."

Don gave Frank a slight nod. "The thing is, you see," said Frank. "We don't see how anyone else could have got on to the site, on to Beans's plot, killed him, and then left again without being spotted. And I presume you didn't see any strangers there that morning?"

She didn't look at him, just stared at her lap. But Don could see her working it all out in her mind, and coming to the inevitable conclusion.

"So you agree then," he said, after a moment's silence, "that it must have been one of...one of you."

The last word caused her to snap back to attention, as he'd intended it should.

"Not Tropical," she said, meeting Don's gaze with defiance.

Don was taken aback. "Not...who?"

"Tropical," she repeated. "Not him."

"Why not him in particular?"

At last she smiled again, though the casual welcome had gone from her eyes. "Well, no reason, except I bet they've all been telling you it was him, haven't they, nudging and winking. What with him being foreign. I know how people get—I used to go out with a black lad when I was at school."

Don decided to take this at face value. "OK then," he said. "Not him; not you. One of the others, in that case."

She shrugged. Don got the impression she'd said her piece, and whatever else they got would just be what she thought they wanted to hear. Pity, he could happily have sat here all morning.

"Well," she said. "I know Beans and Compost Joe didn't see eye to eye all the time."

"Do you know what about?"

"No. They both take it pretty seriously, gardening and that. And there's that family, the religious lot. Spooky lot, they are, to be honest. Anyway, they rubbed him up the wrong way for some reason. And Mr. Perfect, Beans didn't take to him much, and Dill, the American woman—"

"Perhaps they were all in it," Don said, screwing his face into friendly mockery. "Except you, of course." He stood up, thanked her for her time and her hospitality. She said the appropriate words as she saw them out, but when her eyes met Don's he saw in them an absence of warmth, as if he really were a guest who'd disappointed his hostess with his impolite behaviour.

"Anyway," she muttered, as she opened the door for them. "I hope you catch him soon. My husband won't let us go down there again until you do."

TEN

THEY DROVE FOR about ten minutes, in the opposite direction from central London, until they found a pub for lunch that they hadn't yet tried. "As far as possible, always try a different pub every day, Frank," Don informed his pupil. "Essential part of police work, getting to know the local boozers."

At the bar, Frank watched nervously as the DI scanned the hand pumps and optics, but relaxed when the barmaid took their order: "Two pints of Best, please, and a selection of sandwiches."

A beer day, not a wine day, Frank thought; I'm sure that's a good sign. He relaxed even further when Don lit up a cigar. He wouldn't have sworn to it in court, but he was pretty sure his boss neither drank beer nor smoked on his Down days.

"We'll have a word with this bloke, Tropical, after lunch," said Don, opening up his cheese sandwich in search of its alleged pickle content. "Look at that." He held the bisected sandwich out for Frank's inspection. "That is 'with pickle,' that yellow smear is. Looks like someone's gobbed on it."

Frank coughed, and replaced his own lunch back on its plate, half-eaten. His cheese and pickle sandwich had, as it happened, been reasonably well endowed in the phlegm department.

"We know which one he is, anyway," Frank said, checking the lists of names. "Jaime Fernandez, that's the only foreign-sounding name there."

"Say what he does for a living?" This time as he spoke, Don was unpeeling an egg mayonnaise sandwich. He started to say, "Look at that," but Frank was too quick for him.

"Window fitter," he said, loudly enough to turn a few nearby heads.

Don gave him a mildly puzzled look. "And you reckon that's significant, do you?"

Frank shook his head. "No, not particularly. Why?"

"Oh, no, nothing," said Don. "Just the way you said it. You seemed to almost shout it. Not to worry, probably my ears packing up. They say heavy metal music does that to you, don't they?"

Frank kept his mouth shut, refusing to chase that particular hare.

"Interesting, isn't it?" Don swallowed the last of his egg mayonnaise with a grimace. "That Mother Hubbard assumed everyone would be fingering this Tropical bloke, when in fact she's the first person to even mention his name."

"More encouraging than anything, I would have thought," said Frank.

"How do you mean?"

"Well, Mother Hubbard's assuming the worst—you know, racial prejudice and that—and she's wrong. So that's good news, isn't it?"

"Hmm," said Don, lighting another cigar. "Could be. Or it could be that she wasn't just assuming the worst, she actually knows the worst."

"What? Racial harassment on the allotments?"

"Xenophobia amid the zucchini. Why not?"

"I don't know—just doesn't seem the sort of place. The sort of people, I suppose." Frank sipped his pint, and thought about what Don was suggesting, which was what, given the DI's pointed silence, he assumed he was supposed to do. "I suppose you could be right, though, you never can tell."

"Thank you!"

"No, I mean you never can tell about racism, sir. But if you're right, then why didn't anyone suggest Tropical to us as a suspect? If they're all against him like that?"

"No idea," said Don. "Guilt? Embarrassment? Anyway, we can ask him."

Frank was looking at PC Standfield's list again. "We'd best make a start, then—he doesn't live all that close. Take us about fifteen-twenty minutes at this time of day."

IT TOOK EIGHTEEN, and when they did arrive at the West London rooming house given as Tropical's address, it looked as if they'd had a wasted journey. True, a man who appeared to be in his thirties, and of Hispanic origin, did answer the door, eventually, to their hammerings—but he seemed to speak no English beyond the single word, "No."

As they were about to either give up, or make an arrest, depending on whether DI Packham thought the Latin man was being straight with them, a woman's voice on the staircase behind them intervened.

"Who the hell are you, banging on my door? Jehovah's?"

The woman looked like a gypsy, Don thought, a theatrical gypsy, not a real one. What was that opera they were always doing on Channel 4, the one with the cleavage? Anyway, this was that show's heroine, brought to life. Dark, curly hair, and lots of it; flawless, white coffee skin; bright clothes and big earrings. Even the worried eyes and the arms overloaded with shopping didn't spoil the overall effect.

Christ, I could leave home for someone like you, thought Don. If I had anyone to leave, that is.

"Not Jehovah's, love," he said, giving her his best smile. "Far worse. Coppers." He showed her his card.

She froze, and for a moment Don wondered if she was going to run. He bloody hoped not; her legs looked a lot more used to exercise than his.

"Who you are looking for?" she asked, putting her shopping down on the stair in front of her. Nice one, thought Don; that little barricade of groceries could give you an extra three or four seconds in a chase.

"Not you," he said. "Chap called Jaime Fernandez. A window fitter," he added, in case this house was full of Jaime Fernandezes.

It was evidently the right answer, as the woman picked up her shopping and finished her ascent of the staircase. "Jaime? He doesn't live here. He never lived here."

"He's not in any trouble," said Frank. "He was a witness to a crime; we just need to check some facts with him, that's all."

She gave him a tired smile. "He still doesn't live here. He gave you this address?"

"That's right," said Don. "Sorry to bother you."

"No bother," she sighed. "He occasionally sleeps

on my floor, you know? But he has no right to give this as an address. An address is where you live, which is not here, for Jaime. I have a phone number, inside? It's for his mobile.''

"We already have that, thanks," said Don.

She raised her chin at him, pulled down the sides of her mouth. "Pity you didn't call first, hey?"

"As it turns out, madam, yes," Frank couldn't resist saying. Don had told him that he never rang suspects before visiting them, because it gave them a chance to sew their mouths shut before he got there.

Under the circumstances, however, they had no choice but to phone the mobile number. It was answered by a man whose English, while accented, was fluent, and who readily gave them his location—a new cul-de-sac development roughly a five minute drive from the pub they'd been in earlier.

"This used to be a sports field until a few weeks ago," said Jaime Fernandez, aka Tropical, looking around at the new houses on which he was presently employed fitting double-glazing. "At least when they concrete over the allotments I'll get a few days' work out of it!"

Tropical told them he hadn't had lunch yet and invited them to join him while he ate his sandwiches sitting on a freshly built boundary wall. He seemed friendly and open enough: wryly wary, but with the easy manners of a man who has learned that it is sometimes easier on the nerves to expect the best.

Tall, dark-skinned, and ruggedly handsome, he could have been any age between thirty and forty-five. He was slim, just this side of thin—kept this side of it by muscularity, the kind of muscles that come from work, not exercise. There was grey in his short, curly hair, and grey around his eyes. Here was a man, Don reckoned, who had come to terms with suffering; not beaten it, but perhaps arrived at a peaceful cohabitation with it.

"Sorry about the mix-up over the addresses," he said, as he tore a length of French bread, filled with cheese and salad, into three pieces. "I was living with a girlfriend, but we split up. Haven't really sorted out anything permanent yet. I didn't want to give the policeman who asked a No Fixed Abode, you know? He might have arrested me there and then, yeah?"

Don noted, and dismissed, the divergence in the two accounts of his previous living arrangements. Tropical insisted that they each take a piece of the sandwich, and when they had finished eating, Don brought out his cigars. Tropical took one with an enthusiasm which managed to suggest that this was the best cigar he'd ever smoked. Frank took one, too, so as not to seem standoffish. He wasn't much of a smoker, but even so he did not believe this was the best cigar he'd ever smoked.

Tropical told them his life story, in outline. He was a refugee from Latin America, had been in this country nearly twenty years. In theory, he still hoped to go home one day if that should ever be possible, but if not, "Well, life here is OK. I quite like the weather, even!"

"Plenty of work?" asked Don, relaxing in the surprisingly warm spring sunshine.

"Back home I was a time-served carpenter, and a union official. Here, I am a window-fitter, or a window-fitter's mate, really." He shrugged. "It is not such satisfying work, no, but the pay is not bad at all, and they are a decent bunch to work with.''

"Tell us about the allotment, Tropical,'' said Don, deliberately using the man's plot name, to see if it would get a reaction. It didn't, not as far as he could tell.

"The allotment? Best thing I ever did! Been there eleven years now. I love it. Every spare minute I am down there. I was raised the peasant way, you know.''

"Me too,'' Don put in.

"Ah? Then you understand, Inspector, for me to have my own vegetable patch, it is as natural, as essential, as having my own hole to shit in.''

"Of course,'' said Don, who had once had a window box, which he had used primarily for stubbing out cigar butts whilst leaning out of the window enjoying a smoke. His girlfriend at the time had had an allergy to tobacco. "And the people there, on the site—you find them congenial?''

"Well, yes, they come and go over the years, you know, and some of them are friendly, even become friends of a sort.''

"And others?''

Tropical spread his hands. "If they are not so friendly, you don't have to get into bed with them, do you? Just nod good morning, very English, and go back to your hoeing.''

This would have to be asked right out, Don decided. "You've never had any, forgive me asking, racial bother on the allotments?''

"No, not really,'' said Tropical. "Less there than elsewhere, to be true. And you know, I have to say, less here in England, maybe, than back home.'' He saw their raised eyebrows, and laughed. "I know we are all wogs to you, but even amongst the wogs, there are differences, you understand? Rivalries, superiors and inferiors." He laughed again, louder, to break the tension.

"So, it's a good life, Tropical?" asked Don, partly at least because, sitting there in the sun, smoking, talking to an intelligent companion, he thought it was, actually, quite a good life.

Tropical smiled. "I have no complaints about my life here, you know. I don't understand the English, of course, I don't believe I ever will. But then, that's what the English are for, isn't it? That's why they were put on this earth, to puzzle and amuse the rest of humanity, and of course, to give us refuge when we are desperate."

"You're very welcome, Companero," said Don, bowing from the waist.

"Well you know, Inspector, in fact I think I am. Certainly I was made very welcome when I arrived, and so it has been, all things told, ever since. But of course, twenty years ago…" He puffed out his cheeks, and exhaled heavily. "Well, life is a bit different, a bit harder for us all today, who can deny it. I think everything in this country was better twenty years ago, is that not the case, Inspector?"

"I couldn't possibly comment on that, as a serving police officer, Mr. Fernandez," said Don solemnly. "Though you are of course, abso-fucking-lutely right in every respect."

The two older men shared a moment of laughter; the kind that denotes complicity, not amusement, while Frank looked on, from the outside. Don could read the young PC's thoughts on his frowning face: Twenty years ago? Wasn't it all strikes and riots and inflation twenty years ago?

"What about Beans," said Don. "Did he make you welcome?"

"Well, at first, I think, he found it a bit difficult to talk to me. Maybe because I was foreign, I don't know. He was always pleasant, you know, but not, say, overly friendly. But the thing about Beans you got to understand is, he had time for anyone who was serious about the gardening."

"And he could see you were serious, as time went on?"

"As time went on, right. Not crazy serious, not stupid about it. He didn't care much for anybody who got too, what would you say, high-falutin? But if you stuck at it, you grew your crops, you observed the unwritten rules—you know, the etiquette, the manners, the style…well, so, we got on fine. I shall miss him as a matter of fact. Him and me, we were veterans of that place."

"You were friends?" said Don, his head on one side.

Tropical shook his head. "I know what you mean. No, not friends, as such. I never went to his place, he never went to mine. When I had one! We never, you know, went for a drink or something like this. But that's not how it is on the plot, not necessarily, anyway. It's the British way, isn't it?"

"How do you mean?" asked Frank.

"To have different friends for different purposes. Like, this one's a boozing pal, this one's the guy you call when your wife kicks you out, this one is…you know. And Beans and me, we were allotment friends. Yes, I will miss the old bugger.''

On an impulse, perhaps picking up on Tropical's last word, which sounded odd in a Latin American accent, Don said, ''I've heard he was a bit of a nosy old sod, always finding things out about people. Things, maybe, they would prefer weren't found out?''

Tropical stopped smiling, and looked, levelly, first at Don, then at Frank. As if, Don thought, he was just reminding himself what these two agreeable blokes did for a living. ''Only local history, Inspector,'' he said. ''So he had nothing to find out about me, because I'm not from here. Remember?''

''Of course,'' said Don, and then added, because he was sure this interview had gone as far as it could now, ''Care to guess which of your neighbours killed him?''

Serious and quiet, Tropical said, ''No, Inspector. No offence to your profession, but that is one game I do not play.''

And then Don remembered that Jaime Fernandez was, indeed, a foreigner; from somewhere else, from another world.

ELEVEN

THIS TIME, Don used his mobile phone without being told to. Mrs. Ferry informed him that she and her family would be at home, and willing to receive the detective inspector and his colleague, from about five-thirty that afternoon.

In the meantime, Don announced, they would have another look around the murder scene.

There was only one gardener at work on the site when they arrived; not surprisingly, Frank thought—it had turned suddenly cold in the last half hour, the way it will in April, and besides, it was a weekday afternoon. Weed would probably be in his bedsit, keeping warm in his own chosen manner. The Squire was probably putting up some shelves, or being taken shopping under protest. The rest, presumably, at work.

The lone exception was Compost Joe, who called out to the policemen as they passed his plot. ''All right, gents?''

''Quite well, thank you, Joe,'' Don replied, without breaking his stride.

''Have you nicked him yet, then?''

''Who?'' said Frank, detained by the cheery confidence of Joe's question. The DI, meanwhile, walked resolutely on.

"Who?" Joe echoed. "Mr. Perfect, of course. The solicitor."

He really has got a thing about Freemasons, thought Frank. "It's not exactly a criminal offence, is it, Joe? What he's doing? However much you and I might privately disapprove," he added, more quietly.

"Isn't it?" Joe sounded puzzled, but not shocked. "Funny old world," he said, turning back to his composting.

Daft bugger, thought Frank, and hurried to catch up with Don.

They beat the bournes of old Beans's allotment, not looking for anything in particular, as far as Frank could tell. Just looking. All part of the detective's job, he supposed. Fine by me if it keeps the boss happy.

"Wonder what'll happen to the plot?" said Frank, who was becoming suspicious of long silences where Don was concerned.

"Well, assuming the land deal doesn't go ahead, I suppose someone will take it on eventually. And if the land deal does go ahead, then it's an academic question, isn't it?"

"They should get good runners, whoever does take it. Nice drop of blood in the trench."

"I suppose so," Don replied, apparently missing the point of Frank's attempt at CID-style black humour. "There's not many vacant plots here, are there? Must be right what we were told, that allotmenteering's becoming popular again."

"I daresay one of the existing tenants will claim it," said Frank. "It seems to be in a prime spot, well sheltered, but plenty of sun. Right near the tap as well. That's important if you're growing beans."

"What's he got under there?" Don nudged a make-shift plastic cloche with his foot.

Frank understood that as the junior officer it was up to him to look. "Broad beans," he reported.

"Didn't just grow runners, then?"

Frank thought back to his granddad's plot. "If it's true he concentrated on beans, that still leaves him a bit of variety to play with. Runners, French, broads. Others too, I daresay. He hasn't got a greenhouse, so he'd be sowing the French and runners from now up until about June. The broads in November, probably, and again early in the year. Maybe some more about now."

He stopped babbling when he saw from the DI's face just how little interest his lecture was arousing in its audience. "Sorry. You did ask."

"So," said Don, lighting a cigar. "Have we seen or heard anything yet that puts us in mind of a good reason for someone killing him?"

"Not really." Frank wondered if that was the right answer. After all, what did he know about murder cases? There again, he didn't reckon Don was a trick-question, one-upmanship sort of boss. "If you assume that most murders are committed for money or sex, there doesn't seem to be an awful lot of either commodity in this case."

"Hmm," Don replied, and set off towards Compost Joe's plot at a brisk, purposeful, hands-in-pockets march. "Just as a matter of interest, Joe, what was it you and Beans fell out about?" he called, as he drew near.

The sound of his voice evidently preceded that of his footsteps, for Joe jumped out of his skin with surprise. Picking up the aerating tool he'd dropped, he stammered "B-Beans?"

"Yeah," said Don, "you know Beans. Guy that got forked to death."

"Who said we fell out?" said Joe. "What have you been hearing?"

"Nothing much. Nothing important. Only—the way you're prevaricating, I'm beginning to think it *must* have been important. Perhaps we should have you down the nick, discuss it formally?"

"Oh, for God's sake, it was nothing," said Joe. "Just something silly."

"Go on, then." Don made a great show of removing his notebook from his inside jacket pocket. Unfortunately, a thorough patting of all his pockets failed to produce a pen to go with it. But Joe didn't seem to notice, and Frank wasn't going to mention it.

"Well, he wanted this plot off me," said Joe.

"You make it sound like the Wild West, Joe! What did he do? Challenge you to a duel?"

"No, Inspector, he just asked me."

"Politely?"

Joe shrugged. "More or less. At first. By his standards. He wanted me to move to one of the vacant plots. There's only two left now, you see, and they're never going to be let. Not to anyone who knows anything about gardening, they're not, anyway."

There followed a short silence until Frank realised that Joe was waiting for someone to say "Why not?"

"Why not?" said Frank.

"They don't get the light."

"Fair point. So that's why Beans wasn't interested in taking over one of the empties. And presumably he thought light levels wouldn't matter to you, because you only grow compost.''

"But we can't know that, can we?" said Joe. "I haven't done any work on light levels yet. Might be crucial to the entire process for all we know.''

"You can have more than one plot, then?" said Don.

"Yeah, provided they're there to be let. Better that than leave them vacant. The Squirrel's got four.''

"Has he?''

"That's why they call him Squirrel. Because he's nuts about gardening.''

Don frowned. "Are squirrels nuts about gardening, then?''

Frank still wasn't sure whether the DI's occasional lapses into literalism were symptoms or techniques. "But what made Beans suddenly want to take on another allotment?" he asked. "He'd been happy enough with just the one all these years, hadn't he?''

Joe shook his head. "It wasn't that he wanted another one, if you ask me. It was just that he wanted to get me off this one. This is a good plot, this one.''

"And he reckoned it was wasted on you?" Don guessed.

"Suppose so," said Joe.

"But you weren't moving.''

Compost Joe blinked behind his Lennon specs, and scowled beneath them. "Why the hell should I?''

The two policemen wandered off in search of a cup of tea and a bun, to fill the time before their five-thirty appointment.

"I know we seem to be down among the petty motives in this case," said Frank, "but a territorial dispute between mild-mannered allotmenteers—that's scraping the barrel a bit isn't it?''

Don was quiet until they reached the car, then he said, ''I promised to tell you my theory some time, didn't I? So here it is. Nothing is too slight a motive for murder, not once you accept and understand the priorities, the values, of a particular community of people.''

''Like allotmenteers?''

''For instance, yes.''

Frank said nothing but looked sceptical. This was a trick, he knew, which could get right up Southerners' noses.

''Think about it,'' said Don. ''Some people would reckon adultery a pretty trivial reason for murder, but you and I know it's the most common one there is. Or imagine how absurd it is for a person to be killed over ownership of a second-hand book written in a language which neither of them reads, containing stories in which neither of them has any interest—''

''But the book's worth a fortune,'' Frank interrupted. ''That's different, isn't it? The motive there is money.''

''Okay, take politics—most people in this country couldn't give a shit one way or the other, and yet all over the world, throughout the history of mankind, folk have been bumping other people off, assassinating them, stabbing them in bar fights, what have you, all because they vote for a different party.''

''It all depends on what's important to people; that's what you're saying?'' Frank wondered how he could have been gauche enough to express scepticism about such a trite statement of the obvious.

Don nodded. "It's simply a matter of what they value enough to kill for. In other words, all murder motives are the same murder motive."

MR. AND MRS. FERRY opened the door to their smart, 1980s detached house together. That is, literally. They opened the door in unison, and ushered their guests through to the dustless, scentless, welcome-devoid living room, in unison.

Once there, they bowed their heads in unison and invited the two officers to join them in prayers for the soul of their dead brother, Arthur Jones.

Don immediately promoted them to the top of his mental Suspects League, on the grounds that it was a well-known fact that religious maniacs will do anything, with or without a motive, and it was furthermore a well-known fact that anyone who publicly believes in God is a religious maniac.

"We haven't really got time for prayers, Mr. Ferry, Mrs. Ferry," said Don, briskly, not giving the weirdoes time to chip in with the inevitable *There's always time for prayer, Inspector.* "We really need to ask you a few questions. If we might sit down?" He sat down, and signalled Frank to do likewise, without waiting for an answer. Don felt very uncomfortable in this militantly middle-class house, and was determined to take control of proceedings from the start.

Mrs. Ferry redundantly waved the officers towards unrepentantly firm armchairs, while Mr. Ferry opened the door into the kitchen, and spoke softly. Upon his word, two children entered the living room, said "Good evening" to the policemen, and sat side by side on a large sofa which was covered in shiny, gold fabric. Their parents took up their positions either side.

One's a boy, thought Don, and one's a girl, and both are somewhere between eight and eleven years old. But other than that, they have no distinguishing marks or features. Blond, perfect, dressed in frighteningly clean Victorian-style kiddie-clothes; instinctively and overwhelmingly repellent to all righteous humans.

If I had to put out a Stop For Questioning request on this family, either singly or collectively, I'd just tell the lads: Bring in any vacant beams caught loitering.

This would be a short interview, Don decided. He didn't care if they had done it, he wanted out of here and away from these freaks.

"So, how long have you had an allotment, then?"

The question came from Frank. Who rattled *his* cage, thought Don? I'm allowed a bit of thinking time, aren't I?

"We took on the allotment only last winter," said Mr. Ferry.

"We were concerned to secure a reliable supply of uncontaminated food," said Mrs. Ferry, very obviously following her master's lead.

"But more importantly, we wish to spend quality time contemplating God's creation, and to teach our children to have reverence for it," added Mr. Ferry.

"We tend the land as caretakers, as the Bible commands," said one of the children. Don couldn't be sure which one; he didn't see either of them move their lips.

Frank glanced sideways at his boss, swallowed anxiously, and asked the Ferrys, "Do you get on well with the other plotholders?"

"Well enough," said Mrs. Ferry.

"With those who wish to get on well with us," said Mr. Ferry. "We don't mix intimately with them—" *For obvious reasons which don't need spelling out, thought Don*—"but we find them agreeable enough."

"They call us The Family, you know." Mrs. Ferry's words seemed to cause an intensification of the universal beam.

Frank knew what was coming next—he knew Weed's list off by heart now—but he was too slow to prevent it. As he opened his mouth to ask a question, any question, he heard Don say, "Actually, Mrs. Ferry, they call you the Addams Family. There's a subtle difference."

The beam flickered, but did not falter. However, all eight Addams Family eyes turned their gaze upon Frank, and did not stray from him for the remainder of the interview. Don Packham no longer existed in the sight of The Family. He had been excommunicated.

"You knew Arthur Jones, of course," said Frank.

"You mean Old Beans," Mr. Ferry corrected him, with a waggish wiggle of an index finger. "One is not devoid of a sense of humour merely because one accepts Jesus Christ into one's life, Constable."

"That's a yes, is it?" said Don. Frank's tactful avoidance of Beans's plot name irritated him almost as much as Ferry's sanctimonious response.

"He was a simple man," Mrs. Ferry told Frank.

"A good man." Mr. Ferry inclined his head in tribute to his own godly generosity. "Perhaps a little rough and ready."

"Somewhat over familiar with the children," said Mrs. Ferry.

Frank's head snapped up from his notebook. Don opened his eyes. "How do you mean, over familiar?" asked Frank.

Mrs. Ferry coloured, and loosened the neck of her jumper. "I simply mean that—"

"My wife means, Constable, that the rearing of children is a great responsibility, and one does not necessarily wish to expose them to indiscriminate influences."

"Was that what you meant, Mrs. Ferry?" asked Frank. But he was aware that the question, from one so young and self-consciously inexperienced, sounded more impertinent than penetrating, and it was answered only with the tiniest nod.

"You can't imagine any reason why anyone might wish him harm, I suppose?" Frank struggled on, though his imploring glances in Don's direction became more frequent.

"No specific reason, Constable," said Mrs. Ferry.

"Except that, when one looks into the heart of a crime, one will invariably find sin at its centre." Mr. Ferry lifted his hands and fanned the fingers, as if he were holding a book in front of him.

"Blimey," Don mumbled. "That's original! We'd never have thought of that on our own."

"You yourselves hadn't had any run-ins with Beans?" Frank gabbled. "Or with anyone else on the site?"

Mr. Ferry laughed, a sound like sand going down a plughole, and after a beat's pause, the other Ferrys joined him. It didn't last long, and they all finished together.

"When one's life is lit by the Peace of the Lamb, Constable," he said, "one does not engage in run-ins."

"Doesn't one?" said Frank, hoping he had been fast and loud enough to cover Don's muttered comment: *"Northern Ireland."*

"One does not," said Mrs. Ferry, the pronoun sounding more awkward from her than from her husband. "We are all sinners, Constable, and we gain nothing by showing hostility to our brothers."

"You know of no one who bore Beans any ill will?" asked Frank.

"Absolutely not," said Mr. Ferry.

"Mind you," said his wife, "one of the men on the allotments is a foreigner, you know…"

As THEY SAT in the car, Frank felt as depressed as Don looked.

He'd seen him going Down during the course of the interview with the Ferrys, and he reckoned he knew him well enough by now to be pretty sure there was no point in carrying on today.

Only one more plotter to see; he could wait until tomorrow, Frank supposed.

"I'll drive you back to the nick, sir," he said. "Or do you want to go somewhere else?"

"Whatever," said Don.

TWELVE

FRANK PHONED the final plotter—Gerald Wilson, "Squirrel" according to Weed's list—at his place of work, Camden town hall, before leaving home the next morning. Told that Mr. Wilson had phoned in sick, Frank set off for the police station, hoping to find that Don Packham had made another of his miracle recoveries.

But there was no Don in the CID room, or in the canteen. No Don's car in the parking lot. Here we go again, thought Frank.

He decided to check the CID office once more before driving round to Don's flat.

"You still looking for the DI?" said the woman detective he'd spoken to the last time he'd been through this embarrassing exercise. "Afraid you'll have to manage without him today, mate," she continued, amid sniggers from her colleagues. "He's just phoned in sick."

"Yeah," said a male DC. "He sounded right rough, and all. Flu, probably." This turned the sniggers into open guffaws.

What the hell do I do now, thought Frank, leaning against the wall in the corridor outside CID. Report for uniformed duty? Do the interview on my own?

A young DC who Frank hadn't met before came

out of the CID room on his way to the gents, and took pity on Frank. "You know that wine bar in the new shopping centre?"

"Yes?"

"I should try there. But don't say I grassed him up, will you?"

The shopping centre wasn't more than a year old, but the wine bar already looked as if it was past its best days. At a corner table, he found Don. He watched him for a while before making himself known.

The DI was drinking white wine, methodically and without apparent pleasure. At this time in the morning? thought Frank. Is he determined not to make his pension? He wasn't the only one watching the morose detective, he realised. The wine bar's manager stood in the kitchen doorway, anxiety crumpling her face. She could lose her job, too. Just because a Detective Inspector orders you to serve him with a bottle of wine at ten in the morning, doesn't mean you're allowed to do it.

Don wasn't smoking. Not that Frank really needed any further clues as to his boss's mental state.

"Morning, sir." He sat down on a chair next to Don, not across from him; he didn't want to have to meet his eyes. "You not feeling too well, today?"

"Coming down with a bug, I think," said Don, and Frank thanked the Gods of Difficult Superiors that at least this wasn't one of Mr. Packham's silent days. "Or cancer. Could be either."

"Perhaps you should be home in bed, then." Don didn't acknowledge the suggestion. Frank called the manager over and ordered two coffees. On second thoughts, he called her back and made it one coffee. The sooner Don got rid of his illegal wine the better.

When the coffee had been served, he made another attempt at conversation. "So, what next, sir? Any thoughts? I was thinking maybe we should—"

"This old bloke, Beans," said Don.

"Yes?" Frank tried not to sound too eager.

"You think about it, he could have died at any time, couldn't he? Old geezer like that."

"Well, yes, I suppose—"

"So if you think about it, probably better off dying like he did, than hanging on for months in some fucking cancer ward."

This wasn't conversation, Frank realised. It wasn't about the case. He said nothing; sipped his coffee. The coffee was terrible, and cold already.

"It's not worth getting out of bed for, is it?" Don spoke to his own chest more than to Frank. "I'm thinking of jacking it in, anyway. No one gives a toss any more."

"We ought to interview this Wilson man, sir. Don't you reckon? The one they call Squirrel." No reply. "I rang his office first thing; he'd phoned in sick. I mean, that could be significant, perhaps? You know, guilty conscience, whatever."

No reply, though he did think he heard Don sigh at one point.

"So what do you reckon then, sir? Knock him up at home?"

"You do it." Don picked up his wine glass again.

"All right," said Frank, "I bloody will."

He left without paying for his coffee. Let Don pick up the bill. He hadn't wanted the sodding stuff in the first place.

GERALD WILSON'S home address was a terraced cottage, two or three blocks from the allotment site. It was the sort of place that would have suited a well-employed pair of newlyweds where Frank came from, though he knew enough about the London suburbs to realise that here, where the postcode was everything, such a place would probably land a working man with a mortgage he'd take to his grave.

Frank got no reply at the door. Did that mean Squirrel was too ill to get out of bed? Or did it suggest that "off sick" doesn't always mean "off sick"—any more than Don's off sick meant off sick.

Although, come to think of it, Don definitely was off sick; it's just that he didn't seem to know it. There's a nice irony for you, thought Frank as he got back in the car and drove round to the allotments: a man who is so sick he thinks he's skiving when he isn't.

From the gate he could see Squirrel. It had to be Squirrel—a short, completely bald man, very skinny, with thick glasses. Sweating heavily, his skin strikingly pale even from this distance, looking harried as he struggled to wheel a barrow which was much bigger, and evidently much heavier than he was, from one plot to another. Would he say, as so many of them did, that getting an allotment was the best thing he'd ever done?

Well, presumably, since he had four of them: two in enemy territory, at Gate End, the other two up at Tap End. What did that make him, Frank wondered:

a Tap Ender, but perhaps with a foot in both camps? No wonder he looked as if the devil himself rode in that wheelbarrow.

"Good morning, Mr. Wilson?" Frank displayed his warrant card. "I'm Constable Frank Mitchell. I'm investigating the death of Arthur Jones. Wonder if I could have a few words."

Squirrel barely glanced at Frank as he hurried past him, pushing—or being pulled by—the wheelbarrow. "Will this take long?" he panted over his shoulder. "Only I am rather busy."

"It is a murder investigation," said Frank, striding after the short man.

"Yes, of course, I realise that." Squirrel had reached his destination—one of his Gate End plots—and was tipping his load onto what looked to Frank like the makings of a bonfire.

"Well, then," said Frank, "if you could just—"

"It's a nightmare keeping on top of this lot." Squirrel picked up three trays of chitted seed potatoes, and headed off again.

If it's such a nightmare, thought Frank, then why do it? Nobody's forcing you. It's a nightmare entirely of your own making. "Look, hold on a second, will you?" He grabbed Squirrel by the upper arm. "I really do need to talk to you. I'm afraid I must insist."

But Squirrel simply walked out of the policeman's grip, as if unaware that he'd ever been in it, and promptly scurried off in yet another direction, this time carrying a hoe and a bucket. Frank swore under his breath, and followed.

Reaching the third of Squirrel's plots that he had

visited within as many minutes, Frank had an idea, and looked around for the means to turn it into a plan.

"Bloody hell," he said. "Look at those overwintered peas—they're thick with weeds!"

"Oh, don't," groaned Squirrel, covering his eyes with a hand. "I've no time for that now. If I don't get these damn spuds in—"

"Here." Frank took the other man's arm again, and steered him over to the row of pea sticks. "I'll give you a hand. Least I can do, seeing as how I've disrupted your schedule."

Squirrel's eyes were as grateful as a spaniel's, and a little misty in the corners, as he looked on the constable with the kind of fathomless gratitude with which a reprieved murderer might greet the Home Secretary's herald. "Would you?" he said, almost too choked with emotion to speak. "Would you really? You are a gent! Here, hold on a mo—" and he set off at a trot towards his fourth allotment. For a maddening moment, Frank thought he'd lost him again. But then he returned, clutching an opened-out plastic manure sack. "Put this under your knees," he said. "Save your trousers."

And so they set to, the policeman and the clerk, kneeling side by side before the double row of peas, plucking out thistles, couch and sundry, less invasive annual weeds, from which they shook the soil before depositing them in a large, black bucket.

It struck Frank that his granddad would sooner have died—or been hideously maimed, at least—before he'd have allowed a stranger to lay hands on his crops. Once when he'd been laid up with a broken leg, he'd been forced to allow his wife to do some unavoidable weeding of the plot, and had made her bring the weeds back home with her, so that he could check that she hadn't inadvertently removed anything that didn't want removing.

Frank had thought all gardeners—all allotment gardeners—were like that. So how come this apparent fanatic was so ready to accept help? Answer: he wasn't really that keen on gardening. As such. Instead, he was a man driven. Well, that was plain to see. And thus, presumably...what was the word? Sublimating. Gardening like a nutcase, in order to avoid facing up to whatever it was that was really biting his bum.

Which was—what? Something ordinary, like sex or ambition? Or could he be sublimating violence? If so, then he was a good candidate for the kind of killing which arose from flashes of anger, rather than from cold planning. *Murderous vulgare.*

"Clears the mind, doesn't it?" said Frank, pulling, shaking, chucking; pulling, shaking, chucking. "Weeding, I mean. Helps you think."

"Does it?" said Squirrel. "All it helps me to think is how much more of it there is to do."

You're a right bundle of laughs, aren't you, thought Frank. "How long have you been here? On this site, I mean."

"Forty years," said Squirrel, without pausing in his labours.

Frank paused in his, though. "What?"

"Keep weeding!" said Squirrel, and Frank resumed. "I've been here all my life," Squirrel explained. "Pretty well literally. My grandfather had this plot—this one we're on now. My father wasn't interested, but I caught the bug young. Granddad made sure of that.''

"Caught the bug is right," said Frank, careful not to lift his hands from the soil except when depositing weeds in the bucket. "How many plots have you got—four, is it?"

For a moment, Squirrel said nothing. Out of the corner of his eye, Frank saw the man chewing his lip. When he did reply, it was in a tired voice. "It's the search for perfection, do you see? I've taken the other three on gradually, over the years. The thing is, an allotment will never be exactly as you want it to be. So the easiest thing to do, if one plot isn't working, is simply to take on another. And then of course that one doesn't quite work out, either..." Squirrel smiled, for the first time that Frank had seen. It was the wry smile of a man who has just discovered that the Home Secretary's herald is, in fact, working for *Beadle's About*. "Good job this is a popular site, or I'd have taken over the whole lot by now, I imagine."

But if you know perfection's impossible, thought Frank, then why... No. None of my business. "You must have known old Beans forever, then?"

"Yes, of course," said Squirrel. "Poor old soul." But he said it in a throwaway manner, devoid of feeling. As if, thought Frank, he is scarcely connected with human affairs, too preoccupied with the hopeless race against nature.

Looking around him now, Frank could see weeds springing up everywhere.

Squirrel had to be brought to life, he decided, if he was to get anything useful out of him. Time to spring a DI Packham-style whammy on him.

"So, you're off sick today, then?" He held the smirk on his face until Squirrel looked up and saw it.

"So what?" said Squirrel, his hands still for the first time. "Hardly a police matter is it?"

"No, no," said Frank, "I was just saying—"

"What am I supposed to do?" Squirrel demanded, waving his arms around. "You've seen these weeds yourself. Am I supposed to just ignore them, let them take over completely?"

"No," said Frank, trying to calm the storm of defensive anger he'd unleashed. "All I meant—"

"It's that kind of attitude that's put the world in the state it's in today. There was never a weed here in my grandfather's day." Squirrel took a deep breath, and resumed his weeding. "Besides, I *was* feeling ill this morning. I came down here to try and work it off."

"Well, yes," said Frank. "It can be very relaxing, can gardening, so I've heard."

"Then the person who told you that wasn't a real gardener," Squirrel scoffed. "There's nothing relaxing about this lot. Do I look as if I've got time to relax?"

You look like it's about time you were locked up for your own good, thought Frank. "Anyway," he said, "how did you get on with Beans? And with the others here?"

"As little as possible, is the answer."

"How do you mean?" asked Frank, when it became obvious that that was all he was going to get.

"I'm bloody busy here; I should have thought that was obvious. I've no time for chatting and socialising."

"Right, take your point. You haven't fallen out with any of them then?"

"Haven't fallen in with them in the first place," said Squirrel. "Look, the truth is, they all think I'm crazy, the other plotters."

"Do they?" Frank tried to sound astonished by the news. "Why on earth's that then?"

"Why? Because I try to keep on top of my allotments, that's why. Because I'm here at first light, even on working days, straight back here after work, and still here when the light goes at night. All my annual leave is spent here, you know. I've never been abroad—not even to Cornwall, or Blackpool. Can't remember the last time I went to the pictures or out for a meal."

He sounds so bitter about it, thought Frank. As if it's somebody else's fault! Maybe it is—his grand-dad's. Maybe I had a narrow escape when I was a kid. Frank knew he ought to say, So why do you do it then? If you hate it so much? He ought to probe, get a reaction, taunt the poor little nut into giving something away. If there was anything there to be given away. But he just couldn't. Don could've, if he'd been there, but Frank wasn't detective enough yet to use cruelty as a routine tool of interrogation.

Instead he asked him about his job. "Local government, is that right?"

"Yes," said Squirrel. "Camden Council."

"In the allotment section by any chance?"

"Are you mad? No chance! I get enough of that off-duty, I don't have to go looking for it at work and all." The bucket of weeds was full, and Squirrel took it to a compost heap at the end of the plot. When he got back, he said: "No, Finance Department. Very boring, very junior. Suits me. I don't want a job I have to take home at nights."

Another change of tactics, thought Frank. There must be some way of opening up this nut. *Why would anyone want to kill Beans?* obviously wasn't going to work. So, instead: "Was anyone particularly close to Beans, do you know, down here on the site?"

Squirrel shrugged. "Like I say, I wouldn't have noticed."

Oh for Christ's sake! Frank stood up, his knees clicking their message that he was no longer a supple adolescent. "Yes, all right, I understand that. But all I'm asking is, have you seen him with anyone who you thought he appeared to get on with particularly?"

Squirrel seemed not to have noticed that his helper was no longer helping. "Well, that American woman..." he said.

"Dill?"

"I don't know what they call her," said Squirrel. "Big, loud American voice, you know the sort. I believe I might have seen those two in cahoots on occasions."

"Her and Beans? What were they talking about, any idea?"

"How the hell should I know? The Allotment Society perhaps."

"They were both very involved in that, were they?"

"I believe so," said Squirrel. "I don't have anything to do with it myself."

No you bloody wouldn't, thought Frank. "Why's that? Not concerned with the future of the site, Mr. Wilson?"

Squirrel wiped the sweat off his brow with the cuff of a gardening glove. He did look a bit poorly, now Frank came to notice it. "Waste of good gardening time, all that talking."

Frank frowned. "But don't they do all that talking in the evenings?"

Squirrel's shoulders stiffened. "Nothing wrong with gardening in the dark, you know. There's a lot you can do in the dark, if you're methodical about it."

"Right," said Frank. "Yeah, I'm sure there is."

Does he ever sleep? he thought. Or has he got a hammock strung up between the sheds? Perhaps he scores some speed off Weed and keeps going all night. "That's very helpful, Mr. Wilson," he said. "I'm most grateful. How about anyone else? You ever seen any of the others talking with Beans?"

"You weeding or gassing?" said Squirrel, peering up at his skiving assistant.

Fair enough. If that's the deal. Frank knelt down at his station again. "So, how about it? Was there anyone else?"

After a moment, Squirrel replied, "That one they call Mr. Perfect. He's been spending some time with Beans."

Ah-ha, thought Frank. So that's one nickname you do know. What a surprise! "When was this," he said. "Recently?"

"Yes, I'd reckon so. Last few weeks, at any rate."

"What sort of conversations were these? I mean, friendly, joking, arguing, talking about the weather?"

"I don't know," said Squirrel, his voice flat, and Frank realised that he meant it. He really had so little interest in people's doings, that he couldn't even tell whether Beans and the lawyer had been making love or throttling each other.

"So, Mr. Wilson, what do you reckon to all this business about selling off the site? Going to build a hyperstore here, from what I heard." And would that be a disaster or a deliverance for you, I wonder? Maybe both: you'd have to find something else to be nutty about then, wouldn't you?

Squirrel shook his head. "It'll never happen," he said. "There's always talk about development, always has been, ever since I've been here. This is a prime piece of land, every few years someone talks up a storm about flogging it off, building on it. Never comes to anything."

"Sure you're not being a bit complacent?"

"Think about it," said Squirrel. "This is a ward full of mostly well-off, middle-class voters. What politician worth his salt is going to risk alienating that lot?"

So, he does have some connection with the outside world, thought Frank. He does pay some attention to what's going on. At least as far as experience gained in the day job dovetails with his gardening interests.

"Is that the general opinion on the site, would you say? Or is there anyone kicking up a stink about the plans?"

Squirrel looked over at him, and grimaced. "You just won't take *don't know* for an answer, will you? I've told you over and over, I *don't know* what the others are thinking or saying or doing. I don't take any interest, I haven't the time."

Frank said nothing; carried on weeding. This bloke knew more than he let on—perhaps more than he let on to himself. And he needs to keep me talking here at least until we've finished weeding this row.

"That Mr. Perfect," Squirrel said eventually, reluctance in his voice and in the set of his shoulders.

"Him again?" said Frank. "What's he been saying, then?"

"Well, nothing much to me, I don't give him the chance."

"But he's tried to engage you in conversation about the sell-off, has he?" Good luck to him!

"He's hung about here once or twice. You know, sort of wondering out loud about whether there might not be benefits in getting moved to a better site, or the council paying us financial compensation, or whatever."

"I see." So Mr. Perfect was breaking ranks, was he? "And are you tempted? By compensation or whatever?"

Squirrel didn't reply. Frank sighed, erected his legs with disguised caution, and said, "Well, I'd best be getting along. My boss'll be wondering where I've got to."

"Oh," said Squirrel, looking up. "You don't fancy giving us a hand turning that muck heap, do you? Only it looks like rain later; I'll never get it done on my own."

Frank laughed. "If you think of anything else to tell us, give us a call. Then we'll see about the muck heap, maybe."

"Too bloody late by then," Squirrel muttered.

Walking back to his car, Frank had the feeling that, although there was nothing about Squirrel which exactly screamed *Motive!*, nonetheless this was obviously a man living under tremendous pressure.

A man on the edge of snapping? If so, who knew what he might be capable of?

THIRTEEN

THERE WAS A car parked next to Frank's, and as he drew closer an arm emerged from the driver's window and gave him a clenched fist salute.

Don.

"All right, sir?" Frank squatted by the car.

"Couldn't be better," said Don, turning the clenched fist into a thumbs-up. Frank hid a smile, reminded of his and Debbie's "Don Signals." "Bit of a headache this morning, but it's cleared up now."

"Glad to hear it." As he climbed into Don's passenger seat, Frank felt quite dizzied by the speed at which the DI's moods seemed to swing. Though perhaps, he reflected, that was how Don had been able to hold down his job for so long. He didn't go into week-long Ups or Downs; they only lasted a night, or a morning. Not usually long enough for him to get into a fatal mess on the Job.

There again—a morning or a night was quite long enough to get married, or resign, or join the Foreign Legion. Or the Young Liberals. Ice water swirled in Frank's guts as he added something else to the list of activities which Don would have plenty of time to carry out during one of his depressions: presumably, he just wasn't the suicidal type, or else he'd be dead a hundred times over by now.

"So," said Don, lighting a cigar. "You've sorted out the Squirrel, yes? Good man, well done."

Frank gave him a report on his interview with the hyperactive Mr. Wilson. "He's a funny fellow, Don, no doubt about that, but…well, I'm not sure any of it takes us very much further forward."

"Nonsense," cried Don. "Nonsense, that's excellent work. It all takes us further forward, doesn't it? Wouldn't be any point in doing any of it, otherwise."

"Well, yeah, in principle, I suppose. As far as elimination and—"

"Everything matters, Frank. Everything!" said Don, disconcerting the constable by taking his knee in a brief, but nonetheless vice-like, fraternal grip. "All is interconnected, you see. The interconnectedness of all things, Frank, that's what a detective has to keep in mind. One measures a circle beginning anywhere, after all. Who said that?"

Frank resisted the temptation to reply, "You did." He didn't really feel they had that kind of relationship. More to the point, he wasn't really sure he wanted them to have that kind of relationship. "Sherlock Holmes?" he guessed, instead.

"Could be, yes, could be," said Don, nodding. "Sounds like one of his. But whoever it was, he was a wise man. Everything relates to everything else, nothing is complete unto itself. Every single thing has to do with every other single thing. You see, Frank, each and—"

"Right," said Frank, who reckoned he'd got the message. "And as far as—"

"And I'm not just talking about this case," Don continued, slapping the dashboard for emphasis.

"Let's say a man farts in China. And another man wins the Nobel Prize for Peace in—" He stopped, frowning. "Where do they give out the Nobel Prizes, Frank?"

"No idea," said Frank, who at that moment would sooner have died than said Stockholm.

"Well, anyway, doesn't matter. The next bit of this particular circle that requires measuring is the bit with Land Deal written on it. I feel very strongly that that lies at the heart of the whole case. Wouldn't you agree?"

Frank was still having trouble getting used to the idea of a superior officer who wanted to hear your opinion when he asked for it. "I think I would, as it goes," he said. "It's something people are likely to get steamed up about, at any rate. And it seems like there was by no means unanimity about it on the site."

"Exactly," said Don. "And Beans was at the centre of it."

"So we're off to talk to the developers, are we?"

Don smiled. "Well done! That's exactly where we're off to. While you were chatting up the nutty Squirrel, I was on the phone to the town hall. The chairman of the Disposals Committee—do you like that? Disposals? That's their euphemism for privatisation. Anyway, the chairman is a dedicated public servant by the name of Councillor Piers Adam. Never trust a man whose surname is also a first name, Frank."

"I won't, sir," Frank assured him. "Although in fact, I believe Mitchell is not unknown as a Christian name in parts of America."

"America doesn't count," said Don. "Everything's

a Christian name in America. Doorknob's probably a Christian name in America. Mobile Phone's probably a Christian name in America.'' He looked around for inspiration. ''Fluffy Dice is probably a—''

Fluffy dice? I wouldn't have you down as the fluffy dice type, thought Frank, turning in his seat to look at the back window—the dice-free back window.

Don laughed until Frank feared for his continence. ''Gotcha there, Frank! Made you look, made you stare, made the barber cut your hair!''

''Absolutely,'' said Frank. He wasn't sure which was worse, in some ways: Don Up or Don Down. Seeing him Down could be frightening, but then when he came back Up—well, look at the daft sod. And at least this was in private; all in the family, so to speak. God only knew what outrages he might be unable to contain in the presence of the Chairman of Disposals. ''So where will we find Councillor Adam, then?'' he asked, when he was once again able to make himself heard over Don's wheezings and cries of ecstatic pain.

''Ah,'' said Don. ''He's not on council business to-day, and thus presumably is going about his business at his place of business. He's the senior partner in a firm of solicitors, surprise surprise, in the town centre.'' He turned on his ignition. ''So, if you want to follow me, Frank…''

Don waited for the PC to get out of the car, but the PC didn't budge.

Even if Don does have a superhuman metabolism, the PC was thinking, and granted that he doesn't seem at all intoxicated, he must still be over the limit. He was drinking white wine for breakfast, for God's sake!

They were in plainclothes, in an unmarked car. Supposing they got stopped and breathalysed?

"I was thinking, actually, Don. Mightn't it be better if we both went in the same car? So we can chat on the way, like?"

"Good point, yeah," said Don. "You'll have to drive, mind—I don't like talking and driving. Do you mind?"

"Not at all," said Frank. "My pleasure."

The receptionist at Adam, Adam, Silk was a well-developed woman of about forty, who seemed to take an instant liking to DI Packham. She was a bit too blowsy for Frank's taste—bit too much lipstick, and the way she wrapped both her legs around the shaft of her swivel-chair, so that her left side was about two feet nearer the ground than her right side, struck him as unnecessary in one so amply cleavaged. But each to their own, he thought.

On what was almost visibly a whim, Don asked her if Mr. Silk was available.

Chewing her lips even as she spoke, the receptionist replied that Mr. Silk was deceased.

"I am most terribly sorry, Miss," said Don. "My condolences to you and to all who loved him."

She giggled. "Died ten years ago, before I started."

"I see," said Don. "Very well then. In that case, might I possibly have a moment of Mr. Adam's time?"

The receptionist took a moment to hand iron a few creases out of her blouse, and to catch up on some urgent lip-chewing, before she replied, "Mr. Adam retired two years ago."

"Ah," said Don. "How about Mr. *Adam*, then?"

"I'll tell him you're here," she said, and wiggled off in the direction of the private offices.

Don watched her movements with undisguised hunger, and then turned to Frank with a roguish smile. "You can't beat the Marx Brothers, can you, Frank?"

"Indeed not, sir," he replied. "Especially when it comes to the old dialectic."

The receptionist reappeared, beckoning, and the three of them—Don, Frank and Don's guffaw—followed her through a door marked Piers Adam.

DON FELT HIS prejudices uncurling as they entered Councillor Adam's office. Plush, was the word for the room. And, as far as Don was concerned, slimy was the word for its occupant—a shiny-faced man of about fifty, wearing a good suit and too much expensive cologne.

And a wary expression. "CID officers? I can't imagine what you might want to see me about!" The lawyer spoke with an attempt at joviality, but Don had the distinct impression that he *could* imagine what they might want to see him about.

"It's in connection with the death of a man at the Crockett's Drive allotment site, Councillor."

"Ah—yes. Yes, of course." Adam's tension drained from him, before their eyes. "Yes, bad business. I heard about it on the local news, of course. Coffee?" Without waiting for a reply, Councillor Adam purred an order into his intercom. The coffee arrived almost immediately, wiggled in by the receptionist. "Yobs, I suppose, was it? Crack addicts? From the council estate, no doubt."

It's still a "council estate" to him and his kind, Don

noted, no matter who owns the houses. "Oh, bound to be, sir," he said. "Bound to be. But for now we just need some background, you understand? Got to go through the motions."

"Absolutely, Inspector," said Adam, all bonhomie now that he knew he was dealing with a man of the world. "Fire away."

"Thank you, sir." Don made a pretence of consulting his notebook. "Now then—of course, you must have known the deceased, Mr. Arthur Jones?"

Adam swallowed some coffee the wrong way. "Me? What? No, no, I don't think so. Why would—"

"He was chairman of the tenants' group, sir," said Frank. "On the allotments. The ones you're planning to sell."

"Oh, was he?" the councillor replied, his eyes wide. "Yes, right you are—the name does ring a bell, now you come to mention it. Thing is, you see, it's mostly officers of the council who deal with that side of things, rather than elected members. My colleagues and I are more at the *conceptual* end of things, as it were."

"Of course, sir," said Don. "I understand. You're a busy man. Tell us something about your development plan for Crockett's Drive. You've been meeting some resistance from the gardeners there, I believe?"

Adam wrinkled his nose, dismissively. "Well, you know, one always encounters a few dinosaurs, doesn't one? Types who still think the state owes them a living."

"Oh, yes," Don agreed, with a matching nose wrinkle. "Quite so."

"People don't always appreciate progress, Inspector. Especially those who can't make the grade."

Don joined in the councillor's sad smile. "Quite, quite."

Adam studied Don's face for a moment. "Don't think we've met, have we, Inspector?" he said quietly, rubbing his thumb across his palm.

Don winked—he hoped winking was an approved Masonic greeting ritual—and replied, "I don't believe we have, Councillor, no. But I'm sure we shall."

Catching Frank's eye, he gave him a wink, too. So, you think I'm laying it on a bit thick, do you, Constable? Well, the councillor doesn't seem to have noticed, does he?

"What improvements exactly are you planning for the site?" Don asked.

"Ah, well," said Adam. "I can't be too specific, as you'll appreciate. Commercial sensitivity, and so on. But I can tell you that it will be a mixed development, including some housing, offices, one or two leisure facilities."

"Sounds splendid."

Adam smiled modestly. "It'll mean prosperity for all, Inspector, I have no doubt of that."

And votes, thought Don. And money in certain back pockets. Tropical was right—this country has turned to shit in the last twenty years. At least in the old days, bent politicians had the decency to be furtive.

"But the plotholders are giving you some trouble, yes?" he said, his manner one of friendly concern.

Adam looked smugger than ever. "Not all of them, Inspector. Not all, by any means. I am confident that this slight problem will soon be solved."

"Is that right?" said Don. "Will you have to spend out much in compensation?"

"One trusts not. We are offering them relocation, naturally."

Yes, thought Don: to an inferior site which will itself be privatised next year or the year after, no doubt.

"Or monetary compensation, as you say," Adam continued. "And you know," he gave a dry chuckle, "the local Sainsbury does do a very good line in imported organic produce. So what's their beef?"

Don shook his head. "Dinosaurs, sir, as you rightly say. You don't anticipate your current difficulties being long-running, then?"

"Not at all."

"What about the laws governing allotment provision by local authorities? Don't you have some kind of statutory duty?"

Councillor Adam's delight in his own cleverness had now reached such a pitch that he was starting to wriggle in his seat. Funny, thought Don, but his wriggle isn't nearly as attractive as his receptionist's.

"The laws, I am glad to say," Adam replied, "are gratifyingly vague. Drafted with real foresight!"

"Then it's full steam ahead, Councillor?" said Don. "You certainly seem very confident that the allotment holders won't be more than a passing irritation."

"Let us put it like this, Inspector," said Adam. "I have received certain…intelligences. Now, I really can't say more than that."

"Quite so," said Don. "Point taken." As he shook hands with the councillor, he twisted his fingers about in a random, but immensely elaborate parody of a ritualistic handshake.

Let him chew on that one, he thought, imagining the lawyer spending the rest of the afternoon consulting cabalistic tomes to try and discover just what manner or rank of mega-Mason his new friend might be.

"It's the land deal," said Don, almost before Frank had a chance to get into the car and close the door. "I was right. That land deal is at the bottom of it."

"Can't argue with you there," said Frank. "Given how obsessive most of these plotters are about their allotments, it's the nearest thing to a rock solid motive we've seen so far. And, best of all, it doesn't require heaps of psychology to hammer it into place."

Don lit a cigar, nodding with enthusiasm all the while, so that it took him a moment or two to line up the cigar with the flame.

"Not only that," said Don, radiant, "but we've got a proper suspect now."

"Yeah," said Frank. "If that tosser, Councillor Adam, isn't behind it all, he bloody should be."

Don shook his head. "No, Frank—right motive, wrong tosser. All that Masonic crap, it suddenly made me realise what was going on." He nudged Frank impatiently, and pointed at the ignition. "Come on, mate, don't hang around. Let's go and arrest Mr. Perfect for the murder of Old Beans!"

FOURTEEN

FRANK DROVE as slowly as he could, given that every time he reduced his speed to meet a red light he got a jab in the ribs and a cry of "Go on! We're coppers, for God's sake!"

Still he persevered. He knew he was going to need every spare second he could squeeze from the journey to persuade Don that an arrest might, at this stage, be mildly premature.

"It's him, Frank. It bloody is!" said Don, drumming his knuckles on the dashboard in frustration as the refuse lorry in front of them sauntered down the narrow street at minimum cruising speed. He stuck his head out of the window. "Bloody privatised bastard, get a fucking shift on!"

"I'm not arguing with you, Don," said Frank, referring to the murder investigation rather than to the privatised bastard. "All I'm saying is, let's interview him again, armed with our new knowledge, and see where that gets us. Don't let's show our hand too early." Since we haven't actually got a hand to show, he added silently.

"We should have listened to that Compost Joe," said Don. "Or at least asked him what he meant."

"Sorry?" Frank eased past the privatised bastard as

slowly as possible. "What's Compost Joe got to do with it?"

"Don't you see? We kept thinking he was telling us that Mr. Perfect was a Freemason, yeah?"

"Yeah..."

"And we weren't greatly interested, we just thought he'd got a bee in his bonnet about secret societies. Right? But what he was actually telling us, was not that the solicitor's a mason—Christ, all solicitors are that, half the country's in the Masons, that's what makes it so farcical, it's no more an exclusive brethren than the National Trust. No, what Joe was trying to tell us, and what he assumed we already knew, was that the solicitor was a solicitor!"

"Eh?"

"That Mr. Perfect, in his professional capacity, is working for the developers."

Frank thought back. Yeah...actually, it did make sense. "So all that rubbing his fingers together—"

Don nodded, folded his arms in triumph. "And that mime behind his back, right! We thought he was showing us funny handshakes; in fact he was showing us backhanders. A frequently related, but nonetheless significantly different phenomenon."

Frank thought some more. If Mr. Perfect was indeed a spy, working for the developers amongst the plotters—well, that'd certainly explain why he had no apparent interest in gardening. And, if Beans found out about Mr. Perfect's undercover role and confronted him with it, it was certainly not unimaginable that such a confrontation might end in pushing and shoving. And manslaughter.

Yes, no way round it: the DI really could be on to something here.

"It all sounds good, Don," Frank said, trying to sound enthusiastically cautious. Or cautiously enthusiastic, he wasn't sure which. "But how about, before we nick Mr. P, we have another word with Compost Joe? After all, if he found out about the solicitor spying on the plotters—assuming that is what he was doing—then who knows what else he might be able to tell us? And forewarned is forearmed, right?"

Don scratched his head, quite vigorously, for about thirty seconds. "Yes, all right, Frank," he said at last. "Joe first, then Mr. Perfect."

COMPOST JOE wasn't on his allotment, so they drove to the address he'd given in his original statement. This was a tiny, virtually gardenless terraced house, on a development that was obviously new, but ageing fast. It was also, Don reckoned, about a fifteen-minute walk from the tube station. Every extra minute meant five grand off the price, he'd read somewhere. Or every five minutes meant a grand, or something like that. Not that he gave a sod, personally; he wouldn't have a terraced house in suburbia if they gave them away with the cornflakes.

The woman who answered Don's ring on the doorbell looked somehow older than she looked. Just like the development she lived on, Don thought, you could see what age she was meant to be…but there were more cracks and subsidence than you would have expected.

"Ah, I'm sorry, madam—I fear we may have the

wrong address. We were looking for a Mr. Joe Whiting?''

Joe appeared at that moment behind the old woman, looked over her shoulder to see who the visitors were, blushed, and shooed her away from the door. ''That's all right, Ma, I'll deal with this.''

Joe hurried them through to the kitchen, where, even as he filled the kettle and put it on to boil, he launched into an almost frantically defensive account of how his current domestic circumstances came about. There was nothing of the interesting eccentric in him, Don noted, now that he was far from his natural element, the allotment; now he was just a grown-up man with receding hair who still lived with his mum.

''Sorry it's a bit cramped in here,'' said Joe. ''It's only meant for one, really. My mother rented it when she split up with my dad.''

''How long have you been here, Joe?'' asked Don.

''Me? Oh, Christ, I don't live here. Well, that is, I'm just camping out here, if you see what I mean, while I look for somewhere else. When I got made redundant I couldn't afford to keep my own place on, so I thought I'd stop here for a while. You know, keep the old girl company.''

''Right,'' said Don.

''Just temporary,'' said Joe.

''Right.''

''Now,'' said Joe, peering around the kitchen as if he'd never seen it before. ''Where does she keep the tea bags? Mum! Where do you keep the tea bags?''

You're overdoing it, Joe, thought Don. And as it became clear that Joe's mother wasn't going to reply to his shouted question, Don began to feel quite embarrassed on the poor man's behalf.

"Ah, here they are," said Joe, opening a cupboard. He put tea bags into three mugs, poured on boiling water, got milk out of the fridge, and, without looking, snatched the sugar jar from its hiding place behind the cereal packets.

"What's this, Joe?" Don took a small plastic tub from the fridge door, which Joe had left swinging. The tub bore a hand-written label "Calendula Cream."

"Dunno," said Joe. "Mum's muck."

"Dill's muck by any chance?" asked Don, remembering the American plotter's little sideline.

"That's right," said Joe, taking the pot from Don, opening its lid and sniffing the contents. He grimaced, and added, "A bribe, I suppose you'd call it. She was being very nice to me at one point, when she wanted my vote on something at the Allotment Society."

"Right." Don took the tub back and sniffed it: smelt quite pleasant, actually. Joe's grimace must have been for show—didn't want people thinking he was the kind of person who found cosmetics smells acceptable, just because he lived with his mum.

Not that Don could blame him, really; about a month previously he'd been called to an incident in which a man of twenty-nine had been beaten half to death by three neighbours, who suspected him of being a child molester. Under questioning, the two men and a woman admitted that there had been, as far as they knew, no molestations of children in the area—but pointed out that the young man lived with his mother, had no job or girlfriend, and collected model aircraft. They had been astonished, genuinely amazed, when Don charged them. "It's time you got tough on the villains, not the victims," screamed the woman, just before spitting in his face and kneeing him in the balls.

"So this is the famous Dill glop, eh?" Don said, making a conscious effort to be friendly. "Is it any good?"

Joe laughed. "You've seen my mother!"

True, thought Don—but then having a grown-up son living at home is enough to age any woman.

To business. "Joe. You tried to tell us something the other day about Mr. Perfect, the lawyer, but unfortunately we got our wires crossed. Do you think you could tell it to us again now. I mean, really spell it out for us—imagine we're, say, a couple of thick bobbies who can't tell marg from butter."

Joe grinned. "All right, words of one syllable. Mr. Perfect is, basically, an undercover agent, a solicitor provocateur, working for that Councillor Adam, the bent bastard who's trying to buy the allotments."

"Right." Don let go a deep breath. "So what was all this business with the hands?" He mimed Joe's mime.

"Well, you know," said Joe. "Palms being greased. Bungs being pocketed. Large drinks being taken care of." Suddenly his face fell, and he slammed his tea down on the kitchen counter. "Hey—you're not here to do me for slander, are you?"

Don shook his head, held up his hands in placation. "No, Joe, don't worry, mate. Not our department."

"I should bloody hope not," said Joe, as indignant as if the answer had been yes; such is the power of fantasy, Don thought.

"So tell me, Joe—how do you come to know this about Mr. Perfect? Was it general knowledge on the site?" *Please answer no, Joe.* Because if it was general knowledge, of course, it wouldn't make much of a motive for murder; you couldn't threaten to reveal a secret that everyone knew.

But for a moment, he wondered if he was going to get an answer at all. Joe's face imploded again, his gaze fell to the floor, and Don could almost see his ears pricking, in fear of that most terrible of fates— the mother coming in to humiliate him.

"Joe?" said Don, gently. "This is very important information, and I really do need to know where it came from. I wouldn't ask otherwise."

"My mother," said Joe; at once, so quietly that they could hardly hear him, and so bitterly that Don fancied they would have felt the words from the other side of the street.

His mother? Oh shit, if this was just old lady gossip... But hold on, how come his mother had even heard of Mr. Perfect? "Go on, Joe," Don urged.

Compost Joe sighed, and brought his eyes level with Don's. "My mother," he said, in crisply-bitten syllables, "is a cleaner."

"Nothing wrong with cleaning," said Frank, his voice piping momentarily, reminding all present that you can take the Geordie out of Newcastle, but you can't stop him sounding like a ship's whistle when he's agitated. "Honest work, that is." He blushed and fell silent again.

Well, well, thought Don, that came from the heart. Can't be the wife, must be the mother.

"Joe," he said, but making it clear with his eyes

that he was addressing Frank as well. "Everyone's mother works as a char at some time or another. It's an inevitable part of life on this planet. Isn't that right, Frank?"

"Nothing wrong with cleaning," said Frank.

It wasn't quite the answer Don had been looking for, but when he capped it with "Course there fucking isn't," the obscenity seemed to melt Joe's tension.

Smiling ruefully, Joe said, "My mother was the cleaner at our school. You want to try that, Inspector, if you want to know what embarrassing means."

"Christ!" said Don, before he could stop himself. "Yeah, that would be embarrassing. Point taken. So your mother does for Mr. Perfect now, is that right?"

"Used to," Joe nodded. "And the point is, this guy Mr. Perfect—Jeremy Morgan—he used to work for old Mr. Adam. That's Councillor Adam's father, right?"

"And your mum used to work there, as well? At Adam, Adam, Silk?"

"Exactly," said Joe. "Morgan wasn't a partner, you see, he just worked there. Some sort of junior lawyer, I don't know. Anyway, when he left, my mother went to work for him for a while, but it didn't work out."

Don wasn't going to ask why not. "So Morgan defected, did he? Set up shop on his own?"

"Well, no, this is it. Apparently, although Morgan is legally, technically, a one-man band, he gets just about all his work from Adam, Adam, Silk. His independence is in name only; he's basically a subcontractor."

"So why the pretence?" asked Don. "Why not just carry on working at the firm?"

"You don't get it?" said Joe. "Think about it—this way, they could, for instance, represent both sides in a divorce without anyone knowing."

"Anyone except the cleaner," said Don. "Yeah, I see what you mean. Could be very profitable. And how did your mother put two and two together—how did she connect her Mr. Morgan with your Mr. Perfect?"

Compost Joe's embarrassment returned, full flush. "Well, you know, she came down the plot one day…"

"Right," said Don, keeping his voice neutral. She'd have been down there to take his sandwiches, no doubt, or to make sure he was wearing a vest.

"And she saw him there. He didn't see her," Joe continued, "but she recognised him. And that evening she warned me not to have anything to do with him, to keep clear of him."

"Why would she say that?"

"Because she knew him for what he is—a sneaky bugger."

"She assumed that he was up to no good on the allotments?" said Don.

"Of course—why else would a bloke like that be there? He's not exactly the type you'd expect to find on an allotment, is he? Stuck-up twerp like that."

"Isn't it possible he's just developed an interest in gardening?" said Frank. "Or healthy eating—there's lots of concern about that sort of thing these days, among the professional classes."

Joe was adamant—if Jeremy Morgan was renting an allotment, just when the land deal was being discussed, he had to be up to something. And Don realised why Joe was so certain: because his mum had said it, so it had to be true. He wondered whether Joe himself understood his own reasoning. He hoped not, for his sake.

"Now, Joe, this is important: have you told anyone else what you've told us? About Mr. Perfect working for the developers?"

"No," said Joe, shaking his head.

"You're quite certain? You didn't mention it to Beans, for instance?"

"I'm certain. I only found out a few days before he was killed. I was going to wait for the next meeting of the Allotment Society and spring it on them there—see what Mr. Perfect had to say for himself caught on the hop. But then, of course, he did Beans in and I never got the chance."

"If that's true," said Frank, back in the car, "it buggers the whole theory, doesn't it? If Beans didn't know about Mr. Perfect, then he couldn't have confronted him with it, so Mr. Perfect has no motive."

"Not so fast, Frank," Don replied. "First of all, we don't know that it *is* true. Perhaps Joe did tell Beans, and now he reckons that's why Beans got killed, so he's feeling guilty about it. Or maybe he mentioned it to him casually, in passing, and he's forgotten he did."

"Well…" Frank was obviously unconvinced.

"Or," Don hurried on, "Beans found out about Mr. Perfect independently of Joe, through some similar method."

"Not his own mother, presumably."

"Yes, very funny," said Don. "But whatever, the point to keep in our minds is this: that Mr. Perfect has a motive for murder—to prevent disclosure of his activities as a spy for the developers. It doesn't matter what Joe knew, or when he knew it, since he wasn't the one who got killed. What matters is Beans. If Beans did know, through whatever means, then bingo. We've found the killer.''

"All right,'' said Frank. "Yeah, that works. Certainly any publicity about what Mr. Perfect was up to could have compromised the land deal.''

"A multi-million pound deal,'' Don reminded him. "At the very least it would have cast a nasty smell over the whole business, excited press interest, perhaps have put Councillor Adam in the shit with his colleagues. Nobody has a bigger yellow streak than a bunch of politicians facing a scandal.''

"I can just about see it for Councillor Adam,'' said Frank. "Like you say, if something went wrong he could stand to lose millions, personally. Maybe even face trial. But was it really so important to Mr. Perfect that he'd be willing to kill for it?''

"We don't know whether he was acting on his own initiative,'' Don said, "either premeditated or not. Or whether he was acting on behalf of Councillor Adam—or indeed, of the wider cartel. But one thing we are certain of, it was one of those plotters who actually did the deed, whoever else might have been involved as conspirators. So, you agree, Frank? Time we brought in Mr. Perfect.''

THEY TOOK HIM coming out of his office.

"Mr. Morgan? DI Packham, you remember me, and PC Mitchell. We'd like you to come back to the station with us and answer a few questions, if you'd be so good.''

"Questions?" The lawyer went puce, and then white, and then puce again. "What about? Are you charging me with something?"

"Is there something we should charge you with?" asked Don.

Careful, thought Frank. He's a solicitor. Let's do this by the book.

"I don't know what you mean!" said Mr. Perfect.

"Some new information has come to light concerning the murder of Arthur Jones, sir. Information which concerns yourself."

"Me?"

"And we'd therefore be grateful if you could help us eliminate some inconsistencies that have occurred. Explain a few things. Shouldn't take long."

After a little more bluster, Mr. Perfect agreed—rattled but not broken, Frank reckoned—and they drove back to the station in silence.

As soon as the tape was running and the formalities dispensed with, Don started in on him. "Right, Mr. Morgan, let's not mess around. We know, sir, that you rented an allotment at Crockett's Drive purely in order to infiltrate the tenants on behalf of your business associates. Correct?"

The lawyer looked uncomfortable, a bit shamefaced, Frank thought, but after an inner debate clearly acted out on his face, he decided to brazen it out. "So what? That's not against the law, is it?"

"Probably not, sir," Don agreed. "Bit underhand, one would have to say. Ethically a little dodgy, perhaps. But then maybe that doesn't bother your friend Mr. Adam."

Mention of the councillor's name drew a definite

response from the suspect—an intake of breath, a deepening of the lines around his eyes. Nothing verbal, though, and nothing which could be subtitled for the benefit of the tape.

"Anyway," Don continued, "I wouldn't know about codes of conduct, not really my department. But as you say, under law—no, no offence has been committed as far as I am aware. Murder, on the other hand...well, that'd be a bit more than a code of conduct job, that one, wouldn't you say?"

Mr. Perfect's reaction astonished both officers. It wasn't fear, it was—fury. That's it, thought Frank, that's what it is. Apoplectic, speechless rage. As if...as if this was the one thing he had never expected to hear from them. Which, unless he's a great actor, is a somewhat disturbing development.

"All right." Frank held out his palms to calm the suspect, as Don almost tangibly sank into a Down in the chair beside him. "Let's not get ahead of ourselves here. You admit that you were acting as a—well, as a spy, an undercover agent, an informer, on behalf of business associates of yours who intend to buy the allotment site?"

With obvious effort, Mr. Perfect struggled to bring his breathing under control. Finally, he said, "I reject your melodramatic terms, Constable. But yes, it was felt useful to have a, shall we say, *voice of reason* amongst the tenants. A reliable conduit to ensure smooth communications between all parties."

"A conduit?" sneered Don. "I've heard it called some things in my time, but—"

"I rented an allotment," said Mr. Perfect. "I kept it neat and under proper cultivation. I was as entitled as anyone else to express a view concerning site matters.''

"And your work involved what?" Frank asked. "Reporting back to the developers on levels of resistance to their plans amongst the plotters? Propagandising on behalf of the development scheme?"

Mr. Perfect sniffed. He was evidently not used to having his activities discussed in pejorative terms. Particularly by junior officers with provincial accents. "If you like," he allowed.

"Did you make any converts among the tenants?" The lawyer shrugged.

"What were you offering, Mr. Morgan?" Frank asked. "Bribes or threats?"

"How dare you," Mr. Perfect replied. "I used reasoned argument." But his anger this time seemed a tame, formal creature compared to his earlier outrage.

Frank was beginning to have more doubts than, as his granddad used to say, "a vicar in a whorehouse." True, he'd never conducted an interview with a prime murder suspect before, but even so he was pretty sure this wasn't how they were supposed to behave. And with no witnesses and no forensics, a confession was just about their only hope. Had Don had a plan, something up his sleeve? Or had he just hoped the man would collapse as soon as the accusation was put to him?

Well, no use asking that—Don was absent for the duration. Frank would just have to press on.

"Mr. Morgan," he began, but the next words— even if he'd known what they were to be—died in his mouth, at the sound coming from Don's mouth.

Or throat, perhaps. He looked at the DI, and saw a

man physically changed by depression. His face matched his mood, dark and unforgiving and tormented. The low, bestial growling only heightened the effect. He looked, Frank thought, like one of those old nazi posters you see on documentaries: the anarchist, looking for babies to eat.

"Let's cut the crap, shall we, Mr. Sodding Perfect?" Don was on his feet now, lowering over the suspect. "You killed that poor old man to shut him up from exposing your grubby little schemes, didn't you? Didn't you, you bastard?"

"Sir!" Frank plucked at Don's sleeve.

Don made a fist and raised it—and then let it drop. "Ah, what's the point? Eh, Mr. Morgan? What's the fucking point? Your sort never get put away anyhow, do you? Might as well all roll over and lick your arses, the rest of us—you lot are above the law, aren't you? Probably a fucking Freemason, anyway. Probably went to school with the fucking CPS prosecutor, didn't you? Tossing each other off in the showers!"

"Sir!" cried Frank again. "The tape, sir!"

He had to stop this. He didn't know how he could, or whether it was already too late, but he had to try. This was all going down on tape—all this blatant intimidation and browbeating, strictly illegal under PACE. If they ever did charge Morgan, then at the very least this would blow the case. And if Mr. Perfect decided to make a complaint—and he would, why wouldn't he?—then that was Don's career finished for sure.

And mine, damn it. And my career.

Don's tirade of hate and despair continued, only occasionally comprehensible, and he took no notice of

Frank's pleas. Frank was about to tackle him physically, when he heard Mr. Perfect whimper.

The lawyer was slumped in his chair, both arms shielding his face, and he was whimpering. He wasn't blustering, getting angry, threatening to complain, demanding to see the duty sergeant or the chief superintendent or the Grand Master of the Lodge.

He was *whimpering*.

He does conveyancing, Frank thought suddenly. He's probably never seen anything like this in his life, not even from the perspective of a lawyer, let alone from that of a suspect in a murder investigation. And besides, Don's rage was easily the most terrible thing Frank himself had ever witnessed.

The tape would never be played unless there was a reason for it to be played. If Mr. Perfect wasn't the killer, and he could be persuaded not to complain…

"Mr. Morgan," said Frank. Don's storm seemed to have blown itself out; after a few seconds of wall-thumping he slammed out of the room. "Mr. Morgan," said Frank again, and this time he got the suspect's attention. "I think what we need to do here is—"

"I've got an alibi," said Mr. Perfect. His face was covered with tears and with impression lines left by his watch and cufflinks. He looked like a little boy who'd been locked in a launderette washing-machine by bullies.

After a long moment of silence in which Frank tried to remember what day of the week it was, and what he was supposed to be doing, he said, "An alibi, Mr. Morgan?"

"An alibi." He wept afresh.

"You...you can't have, don't be daft. You were all on your allotments when Beans was killed. None of you has an alibi; we've been through all this."

"Oh yes I have," said Mr. Perfect, his voice tiny, but determined.

"Well..." said Frank. And then he couldn't think of anything else to say.

"I was smoking drugs," said Mr. Perfect, and Frank had to smother a wild laugh; he didn't think Mr. Perfect could survive two bouts of hysteria in one session. Or one lifetime, probably.

"Smoking drugs, Mr. Morgan?"

Mr. Perfect nodded. Sniffed, wiped his nose on his sleeve. Nodded again, more firmly. "Cannabis resin. With that boy, the one they call Weed. You know him?"

"Yes, we know him, sir. Now why on earth would you be smoking dope with a lad like that? Had they run out of cocaine at the office?" But even as he said it, he knew the answer—and his scepticism began to melt.

"To get in with him, Sergeant."

Now that I've saved him from the Deranged Detective, Frank thought, I've been promoted. "So by smoking a joint with him, you thought you'd win his support for the land deal?"

"Horrible stuff. Made my head swim. I had a migraine two days later, I'm sure that was why."

"And where were you engaging in this illegal act, Mr. Morgan?" Frank tried to sound stern, rather than elated. He'd have to play this hand carefully.

"In the bushes, down by the railway line. The

boy—Weed—he knew a place in there, very private. A sort of den in the bushes.''

Just like those kids' stories, thought Frank. The *Famous Five*. ''And you were doing this when Beans was killed? How do you know?''

''The two of us arrived on the site together. By chance, I mean, we both turned up together. I took the opportunity to talk to him—''

''On behalf of your employers?''

The lawyer nodded. ''And then, well, we went into the bushes. We weren't out of each other's sight from the moment we arrived at the allotments, until—well, until Weed said he had to go and return a tool he'd borrowed from Beans. And that was when he found the body, just a couple of minutes later. So you see—''

Frank held up a hand for silence. He wanted to think this through.

Either it was true, in which case Weed and Mr. Perfect were out of the frame. Or else they had done the murder together, or one of them was covering up for the other for some unknown reason—because he had no doubt that Weed would confirm the story; Mr. Perfect wouldn't have dared told it otherwise. Or one of them had committed the murder early on, left the site, and then turned up again later, as if for the first time.

No, that didn't work; someone would have seen them coming and going, mentioned it. And Weed hadn't had time to commit the murder between parting with Mr. P and raising the alarm.

And as for why Mr. Perfect hadn't mentioned this before—well, that was obvious enough. What was helping a murder inquiry, compared to preserving his good name and career?

Frank looked at him. Yes, he was still scared, still in a state. Calmer, now that Don had gone, but still a desperate man.

Good.

"Listen to me, Mr. Morgan," said Frank. "I want you to wait outside for me, while I go and talk to Weed. If your alibi checks out, then you can go home. You're out of it. And we can forget all this happened, yes? All of it."

"Forget about the drugs? You mean it?" The lawyer's mouth fell slack with gratitude, even as his legs crossed involuntarily, to protect him from the sucker punch he half-expected.

"Forget *all* of it," Frank emphasised. No time for excessive subtlety now. "Forget everything we have seen or heard in this room. You understand?"

"Oh, God yes! Oh yes, yes, I understand. You have my word!"

"OK. Now I want you to wait in that cafe over the road. Right? You wait there, and I'll expect to find you there when I come back. No matter how long it takes."

Now to get him cleaned up before anyone sees the state he's in, thought Frank. That's assuming Don Packham hasn't gone and killed someone at the front desk by now.

FIFTEEN

WEED'S FLAT WAS situated above a rank of shops, in one of Cowden's less impressive mini-precincts. Access to the flats was via steps leading to a balcony at the back.

When the stairs curved into a small landing, Frank was almost knocked off his feet by a scruffy young girl; deliberately scruffy, he supposed, since she seemed clean enough. One of these anti-roads types, no doubt. Her hair was dyed black, but her eyebrows weren't. She wore a nose ring, but no spectacles; she peered at him, as he apologised for being collided with.

"Oh, hi, yeah," she said, a small safety smile curling one corner of her mouth. "You looking for Richard, yeah? Only I wouldn't bother, he hasn't got anything. I just been up there, yeah?"

It took him a moment to place "Richard"—Weed was Weed to him, not Richard Hancock. But once he'd done so, he thanked the girl warmly and carried on up the stairs. So, Weed did sell dope—sometimes at least. Well, that had been a very worthwhile collision.

And when he thought about it, he wasn't even surprised that the myopic girl on the stairs had mistaken him for one of Weed's customers. If all Weed dealt

was a little part-time weed, then she wouldn't need to
be short-sighted to think that a young man in a suit
might be interested. Frank didn't approve himself, but
he knew that plenty of respectable young men in suits
did, indeed, buy cannabis: doctors, bankers and, of
course, lawyers among them.

Weed called "Come in" when Frank knocked.
Frank went in. Weed didn't get up from where he was
sitting on the bed, shoeless, his hair uncombed, his
eyes unfired. *Bloody hell,* thought Frank. He looks
worse than DI Packham.

The flat—or room, really, with a door leading off,
presumably to a bathroom—was pretty bare, the bed
its only major piece of furniture. No telly; a portable
radio-cassette in place of a stereo. Clothes hung on the
walls in the absence of a wardrobe—and in the absence of posters too, if it came to that, thought Frank.
A few books, quite a few ashtrays, all full. You can
see why he likes to get down the allotment.

"You look depressed, Weed," he said, sitting on
the other end of the bed. "Flu coming on is it, or are
you suffering from guilt for not telling us something
that you knew perfectly well we needed to hear?"

"I'm sorry, mate," said Weed. "Constable. I'm
sorry, Constable. I been feeling dreadful about this, I
really feel ashamed. I know I should have told you
straight off. It's been worrying me sick; I was going
to come and see you about it, honest."

"So tell me now," said Frank.

Weed's story matched Mr. Perfect's: how they'd arrived on the site, coincidentally, at the same time, very
early, before eight; how they'd gone into the bushes,
from where they could neither see nor be seen, to

smoke cannabis; how they'd come out after "maybe an hour or so, I don't know, I wasn't exactly clocking my watch, ha ha;" how Weed had gone to return the borrowed sickle to Beans—"and the rest is history, right?"

That was it then, Frank thought. Unless they were in it together, which was bloody hard to imagine, then they were both out of it. Better get back to the nick and spring Mr. Perfect, before he recovers his courage.

"Right," said Frank, standing up to deliver a lecture. "Now listen—"

But Weed interrupted. "Listen, Constable, you've no idea how ashamed I am of how I've messed you around. I'm not that sort of person, I swear I'm not, but you got to understand—I've been done for possession before. And I thought, well, if I admit selling dope to a suit like that, I mean, Jesus!"

"Selling it?" said Frank. "You *sold* him the dope?"

Weed blinked at the daft question. "Well—yeah. Obviously," he said. "Constable," he added, remembering his manners.

"I see. And did this happen often—I mean, was he a regular customer?"

"No, he couldn't stand the stuff. Turned him green. No, it was like a bribe, you know? Three or four times it happened, he'd buy some resin off me, we'd smoke it together, and then we'd be like best mates, ho ho. Prat."

"Why did he want to be your best mate, Weed, any idea?" Because even if Mr. Perfect was no longer a suspect in the killing, who had known what, when, could still be important. Did Weed know about Mr. P's undercover role?

"It's to do with this land deal, I reckon. That's what he always wanted to talk about anyway, what a pukka idea it was." It seemed to strike Weed then that he was off the hook for not telling them about the dope earlier—that the eye of the conversation had moved on. He smiled. "You want to know what I think? My theory is that he was fed up with the allotment, only his wife wouldn't let him give it up. She didn't want him back home, cluttering the place up. So he reck-oned, if only the sale of the land could go ahead, then he'd be free at last, free at last, good God almighty free at last, yeah? Ho ho. Well—stranger things have happened." He sat up, bright and light with the relief of unburdened sin, and began rolling a cigarette.

Frank decided Weed was recovering just a little too well. He took the cigarette makings from the boy's hands, and dropped them on the floor. "Listen to me, Mr. Hancock," he said, his eyes only an inch or so from Weed's. "If you ever come to my attention again, for any reason at all, I will do you. Do you understand? I will do you so thoroughly you'll serve longer than the Birmingham Six. Got it?"

Weed nodded. Yes, he knew when authority was being serious. "Got it, Constable," he said. "Hundred percent received and understood."

I'LL BE GETTING a reputation for this heavy stuff if I'm not careful, Frank thought as he dismissed Mr. Perfect from his perch in the cafe.

"You're in the clear, Mr. Morgan—your alibi checks out. And I have decided, for the time being at

least, not to pursue charges against you for buying a
controlled substance."

White faced and trembling, the lawyer looked on
the point of vomiting with gratitude. "Thank you,
Constable," he stuttered. "Thank you, sir." He got
shakily to his feet, but Frank put out a hand to halt
his flight.

"Just one more thing, Mr. Morgan. Did any of your
bribes find takers? And no crap this time. You know
what I want to hear; so just tell me that and then I will
let you go home."

Mr. Perfect didn't resume his seat. Probably didn't
dare, Frank reckoned, for fear he wouldn't be able to
stand again. There was clearly no fight left in him as
he ran a clammy hand over his sweaty face and replied, "Only one. The rest of them, they're all mad.
Obsessed with those bloody allotments of theirs.
Wouldn't have sold them for ready cash."

"Except one?" said Frank. "Tell me about that
one."

FRANK DIDN'T BOTHER looking for Don to update him
before driving home. He just couldn't face it; with any
luck, the DI would be in a better state tomorrow.

"I'm really not sure I'm cut out for this CID lark,"
he told Debbie, over a cup of tea and a lemon curd
sandwich. "It mainly seems to involve making deals,
cutting corners, bluffing suspects, and covering other
men's backs."

"And that's different from normal police work is
it?" she asked, trying to tease him out of his mood.

"I don't know," he said. "I mean, I think he's a
good copper, Don Packham. It's just that...I don't

know. I seem to have been thrown in at the deep end, and I'm not sure I'm a strong enough swimmer.''

"Well, I'm just glad you're not moody like him." She tried not to sound pointed.

"Much more of working with Don," Frank replied, "and I will be."

When the phone rang at ten the next morning, Frank knew who it must be. Debbie hovered anxiously in the kitchen doorway, as Frank hooked the receiver under his chin and carried on making a cup of coffee. He gave her a crooked smile, which she understood to mean, "Ah well, at least we had a lie-in."

"Don here."

"Morning," said Frank, the neutral greeting he had decided on for use in first-contact situations.

"You know," said Don, "it's a very interesting business, gardening. I don't blame you for being so keen on it."

"Actually—"

"I'm thinking of taking it up myself. Did I mention that? Maybe I'll rent Mr. Perfect's allotment, now he won't be needing it."

"Don't you have to be resident in the borough to get an allotment?" said Frank, adding milk to his cup.

"Do you? Oh. Hadn't thought of that. Never mind, maybe I'll take squatter's rights, then."

Frank knew that Debbie was waiting to receive the thumb signal, but the thing was—he wasn't quite sure yet which way the thumb ought to point. Not Down, obviously; the man was talking, making conversation, using more than one syllable per sentence. But somehow, he didn't sound exactly Up. More as if he was making an effort. So, thought Frank, we learn something new: that there is a third phase, neither Mad Up nor Mad Down but…what? Frank remembered how he felt most workday mornings, and decided that the nearest he could get to labelling Don's new mood was, Normal Human Being who'd rather be on a desert isle but realises that survival depends on interaction.

He couldn't wait to get off the phone and tell Debbie. It really turned her on when he said something clever.

"So what happened in the end with our Mr. Perfect?" Don asked. "Did we nick him?"

Frank explained the situation. He felt unable to mention Don's frightening behaviour in the interview room, and he knew the DI well enough by now to realise that *he* wouldn't raise the subject. Unfortunately, this meant that Frank couldn't give him any reassurance that Mr. Perfect wouldn't be complaining. Tough luck, bonny lad; if you want to hear the good news, you've got to talk about the bad.

"Well," said Don, when he'd heard all—almost all. "I suppose this is good news in one way, since it gives us two less suspects to worry about. We reckon that's straight, do we? Weed and the dope alibi?"

"Got to be." Frank gave Debbie a wink over his shoulder, in lieu of a thumb signal. "I just can't figure those two involved in a conspiracy."

"Agreed. The bad news is that this pretty much destroys the land deal as a source of motive."

"Why do you say that?"

"Because apart from the Addams Family—who we'll talk to again first thing tomorrow; it's Saturday so we should catch them in, take today off, OK?— nobody accepted the developers' bribes. In other words, when we were told that the plotters were divided over whether or not to fight the land deal, that was an exaggeration. In fact, they were more or less united in determination to stay on the site.''

"All right," said Frank. "That does away with Mr. Perfect's spying activities as a motive, yeah. But we've still got the possibility that Beans's interest in local history led him to discover something that might interfere with the land deal—and that's why he had to be got rid of.''

"What?" Don chuckled. "Like an old charter or something?''

"Why not?" said Frank, who didn't think the idea was that amusing.

"How likely is that, Frank? I mean really—when you've got a whole brothel's worth of lawyers as primary dealers in the business? If there's anything to find, they'll have found it already.''

"Sure: found it and buried it. Assumed no one else would dig it up, until along comes this interfering old nuisance, Arthur Jones…''

"OK," said Don. "It's a possibility, I accept that. And if you want to keep digging away at the local history angle, do so. But for now, as far as our main effort is concerned, I say we look for something fresh.''

Frank sighed. "Back to the petty stuff, you mean?''

"If you like," said Don. "Back to arguments, resentments, rivalries, lusts. And the way we pursue that is simply to talk to everyone again. Minus the two you've cleared, we go back to the remaining eight plotters, starting with the family that took from Caesar's what was Caesar's.''

SIXTEEN

THE FERRY HOUSEHOLD, they discovered at ten on Saturday morning, was full of clones. Packed to the rafters with vacuous beams. Overflowing with blond curls and blue eyes, bright but dead.

The Addams Family was hosting a prayer meeting.

"Christ," Don whispered to Frank. "What with this lot on Saturdays, and church on Sundays, I bet the weekends just fly by round here."

The meeting was breaking up as the officers arrived, so while Mr. Ferry was shaking hands and dispensing blessings in the lounge, his wife took them through to the smart, soulless kitchen.

"I can't offer you tea or coffee, I'm afraid," she told Don with scarcely disguised pride. "We do not take stimulants on a routine basis."

"I suppose a stiff Scotch is out of the question then?"

"Right," said Frank, with a haste which would have seemed indecent in most circumstances. "We don't want to disturb your morning more than is absolutely essential, Mrs. Ferry, so let's get down to business. We wondered if you could tell us what exactly is your attitude to the proposed land deal on the allotment site?"

Mrs. Ferry hummed and hawed, casting anxious

glances towards the door to the living room, where her husband was still engaged in the Lord's work. "The land deal?" she said. "Well, I—that is—"

"Let me help you out," said Don. "We are now aware that one of your fellow plotters, acting as a representative of the property development consortium, offered you a financial incentive to support the takeover."

Frank had never seen a fit of the vapours before, though he'd heard the expression. He watched, more fascinated than concerned, as Mrs. Ferry fell to her knees, gasping, praying and fanning her scarlet face with her hands. Then he watched, more horrified than amused, as DI Packham gave her a round of applause.

"Have we got it wrong, Mrs. Ferry?" said Frank. "You seem somewhat offended by our suggestion."

"It wasn't like that at all." She drew a glass of water from the tap.

"Hope there's no fluoride in that," Don said, tut-tutting.

"You make it sound like a bribe—it wasn't like that at all. What a horrid suggestion!"

"So what was it like, Mrs. Ferry?" asked Frank.

"The lawyer, Mr. Perfect they call him, he made it clear that if the development went ahead, provision would be made within its design and funding for a meeting place."

"A meeting place?"

She nodded. "For our group."

"You mean," said Frank, "they're going to build you your own church?"

"Bribe," said Don, lighting a cigar.

"Do you mind not smoking in here, Inspector?" said Mr. Ferry, entering from the living room.

"Sorry, wasn't thinking. I'll just finish this one, then I'll put it out."

A venomous tic ran across Mr. Ferry's face. "Obviously," he said, turning his attention to Frank—who might be a minion, but at least wasn't a nicotine fiend, "under the circumstances we had to balance the spiritual needs of the community very carefully against the merely horticultural."

"What about," said Don, through an imperfect smoke ring, "the spiritual needs of all those people for whom the allotments are precious? A rare opportunity to commune with God's creation?"

Mrs. Ferry gave a small, pained smile. "Well, you know, Inspector, when all's said and done, most of the people on those allotments are...well, they are just a bit...one doesn't like to say, but..."

"I know exactly what you mean, Mrs. Ferry." Don nodded sympathetically. *"Common."*

Mrs. Ferry looked to her husband for guidance, but he'd turned away, shaking his head and muttering under his breath. Or praying under his breath; Frank wasn't sure which.

"Well...yes," said Mrs. Ferry.

"Common as pig shit, some of them," said Don, only just loudly enough for the whole house to hear.

Once again Frank leapt into what would otherwise have been a shocked silence. "Presumably, with Beans dead, there is a greater chance of the land deal going ahead now? He was the main source of resistance, wasn't he—or one of them, anyway?"

Mr. Ferry, who had been staring out of the panoramic kitchen window, turned back, his empty smile firmly in place once more. "Well, you know, Constable," he said. "God does move in—"

"Vicious circles," snarled Don. He left the room, and the house—and Frank, with a brief "Thanks for your help," followed him.

"Well, that was a waste of time," Don said, back in the car.

"I don't know," Frank protested. "We got a motive for 'em, didn't we?"

"What—killing Beans to prevent him, in some unspecified way, interfering with the land deal, so that they get a shack to hold their cult meetings in? Come on, Frank! That's not a motive, that's a fantasy."

"So we're ruling out the Addams Family?"

"No way!" said Don. "No, I like them for the killers—that'd just about make my week, that would, pious little morons. But if it is them, then it's got to be something more personal, more urgent. Sex, or money—big money. Big sex, too, if it comes to that. Not some politician's promise of a hut to keep your Bible in; that's nothing to kill for."

Frank tried again. "But the land deal is still—"

"No, forget the land deal, Frank. Forget it, will you? Or put it to the back of your mind, at least. Listen, the land deal only comes in if we suppose that Beans had to be killed—*had* to be killed, mind—because if he'd lived he would have endangered the deal. Right? But think about it, poor old Beans wasn't much of a shield against a rapacious, well-connected, well-resourced, determined cartel of quango gangsters. Was he? Except in an Ealing film, perhaps. So why kill him, which would at best delay and complicate matters?''

Frank was silent for a moment, following the logic, and finding he couldn't fault it. ''So what you're saying is, it's personal?''

''Got to be, Frank. Got to be. What we have to do now is to find another link, a more personal link, between Beans and one of the remaining eight plotters. Or, better yet, between Beans and each of the eight.''

''Each of them? But—''

''Yeah. Listen, Frank. Assume for a moment that each of them is guilty—each in turn, I mean. And then find the motive, however tenuous. We'll start by having another look round the victim's flat—we know him better now, we might see things we didn't see before.''

But Arthur Jones's flat was just as bare and mute as they remembered it. They found nothing to link him personally to any other Crockett's Drive tenant. The policemen weren't there more than a quarter of an hour, before moving on to the next name on their second-time-around list. ''OK,'' said Don. ''Nothing. In which case, we'll just have to make up our own motives, and try to fit the facts to the theories. Good old traditional police methods, in fact.''

The Squire was, of course, working on his allotment. He saw them enter the site, and hallooed them. ''We'll stick with what we know here,'' said Don, as they approached, ''as regards our notional murder motive.''

''The kerb-crawling?''

''Right. Beans found out about the kerb-crawling,

and blackmailed the Squire with it, so the Squire killed him. OK?''

Don didn't bother with exchanging greetings. ''Now then, Mr. Gorringe. You told us that your kerb-crawling experience was not a secret, and was not something you were ashamed of. Is that right?''

''My God,'' laughed the Squire. ''You still stuck on that?''

''So what we'd like now is some proof of your claim that you used the incident as an anecdote in your after-dinner speeches. Can you provide us with that?''

''Right,'' said the Squire. Driving his spade into the soil, and counting off on his fingers, he listed six people, complete with phone numbers, fax numbers, mobile numbers and corporate titles, all of whom, he assured the officers, would be happy to corroborate his story.

''We'll check,'' said Don, as Frank finished writing the details in his notebook.

''Do,'' said the Squire. ''Please. And if, as a result of you jogging their memories, I get any more bookings, Inspector, you're on for ten percent. Fair enough?''

''Saucy sod,'' grumbled Don, as they left the site.

''Will we check his list?''

''Bloody right we will. Won't do us any good, though.''

''He didn't exactly seem rattled by us, did he?'' agreed Frank. ''Who next?''

Mother Hubbard was pleased to see them—until she realised that they weren't there to tell her that they had made an arrest. ''Oh, dear,'' she said. ''I did hope, because—well, I really do miss my little plot. And my husband still doesn't want me going down there, as long as this maniac's on the loose.''

"I bet the kids miss it too, don't they, Mrs. Rutter?''

She smiled—probably always did at the mention of her children, Frank thought—and started to answer Don's question. And then her face fell as she guessed the reason behind it.

"Oh for heaven's sake, Inspector—you're not still trying to make out poor old Beans was touching up children, are you?''

"You must understand, Mrs. Rutter, we have to eliminate every possible—''

"Look, you can forget all that rubbish!'' Her voice became quieter, Frank noticed, the angrier she got. "A mother knows—I know it's a cliché, but it's true. I would have known. There was nothing like that. If only you'd known that poor old man, you wouldn't— you just couldn't—''

"As I say, Mrs. Rutter,'' said Don. "It's not anything we're actively pursuing, it's just that, to be quite frank with you, we are really no further forward than when we last saw you. So we have to check and double-check absolutely everything, no matter how daft it may seem. I am sorry we upset you.''

She shook her head, clearly not trusting speech.

"And what you've told us does put our minds at rest on that particular question. I'm sure you're right— a mother knows.''

"Not true is it?'' said Frank, once they'd left a near-tearful Mother Hubbard behind. "That a mother always knows?''

Don shrugged. "Maybe, maybe not—academic question, isn't it? We've not got a sniff of a motive from her, not so much as a sniff. Anyway, can you picture her killing anyone?''

''Actually,'' said Frank. ''Yes I can. To protect her children, or her marriage, perhaps.''

Don twisted his lips, impatiently. ''Yeah, OK, anyone can be a killer—but not anyone can keep it secret afterwards. If she'd killed him, it'd be all over her face. No, we've got nothing, Frank. Two down, and nothing. This was not one of my best ever ideas.''

He's on his way Down, thought Frank. So I don't dare tell him what I really think: that it's still the land deal at the bottom of all this, only we've got hold of the wrong end of it, somehow.

''So,'' he said. ''Who next?''

''Christ, I don't know,'' said Don. ''It's Saturday afternoon—let's just go back down the site, and see who's there.''

SEVENTEEN

THEY PAUSED AT the gate to Crockett's Drive allotment site, and surveyed their crime scene.

"All present and correct," said Frank, pointing out the players. "The Squire, Queer Gear, Dill, Compost Joe, Tropical and Squirrel."

"Stupid bloody nicknames," muttered Don. "They're getting on my nerves."

Frank ignored him. "Absent, for various obvious reasons, are Weed, Mr. Perfect, The Addams Family, and Mother Hubbard."

"And Beans," said Don. By unspoken agreement, it was Beans's plot that they headed towards.

"Looks overgrown already," said Frank. "Weeds shooting up everywhere. Or is that just my imagination?"

Don said nothing. Fair enough, thought Frank. You want to leave it to me, leave it to me. One day I'll be your superior officer, so I might as well start getting the practice in now.

"We'll start with Queer Gear," he said, deliberately making it a statement, not a question. Don remained silent, but followed him over her plot.

"Afternoon," said Frank.

"Constable, nice to see you again." Queer Gear took off her gloves and wiped a hand on her jeans ready for shaking. Then she looked behind Frank at Don, and put her hands in her pockets.

Tactful woman, thought Frank. "Bit quiet for a Saturday."

"It is," she said, sadly. "But I hear there's already been someone looking over Beans's old plot. They don't stay vacant for long round here, not these days."

"Life goes on," said Frank.

She smiled. "More or less."

Frank really had no idea how to proceed. He didn't think for a minute that this charming, lively lady novelist was their killer. They hadn't come up with any kind of motive for her at all, always allowing for the fact that there could well be some secret which hadn't yet come to light. Produce competitions: that was the nearest they'd got to a motive.

Better get on with it, then: offend another innocent civilian. It's a fun life in today's CID.

"You'll be getting ready for this year's competitions soon, I imagine?" he said.

Something behind her eyes told him that his innocent tone hadn't fooled her. She didn't believe he was here for a casual chat. "Well, beginning to think about it, yes. I suppose so," she replied.

He pressed on. What else could he do? "I remember from my granddad's plot, when I was a kid, how seriously some competitors take these things. He was a leek grower. Never won anything, though, as far as I recall."

She smiled. "Well, Newcastle and show leeks—axiomatic, isn't it? It's not quite as exciting down here, I'm afraid."

"Ah," he said. And then chewed at his lips as he tried to conjure up what he might say next.

The tension sagged from Queer Gear's shoulders as she took pity on the young constable. "Look," she said. "I know what you're driving at, and I don't blame you for it a bit. Got to cover every possible angle, haven't you? But, if it's any help to you at all, I should tell you that I only enter in the more exotic classes. Garlic, peppers…"

"Scorzonera?" said Frank, with a grateful smile.

"Exactly! They don't call me Queer Gear for nothing, you know. Whereas Beans only entered—well, beans. French, runners, broads. Did very well with them too. But you see, there was no direct competition between us at all. And neither of us was ever in the running for the overall trophies, like Best Kept Plot."

"I see," said Frank. "Thanks."

"And you can check that, as well. The competition's run by the council; they must keep records somewhere."

"Thanks," he said again. He looked round at Don—no, still no help there. The DI was standing at the far edge of the allotment, staring off into the sky. "Well then…I don't suppose you've had any further thoughts yourself, have you? On who killed him, or why?" With Don on another planet, Frank felt that this woman was his only ally.

But she shook her head. "Afraid not, no. Nothing. So perhaps I'd better stick to the literary stuff after all, eh?"

"I'm sorry?"

"Literary fiction," she said. "Not whodunits."

"Oh, right. Yes. Right then, I'll leave you in—"

"The only thing that did occur to me," she interrupted, "is that from what I hear on the grapevine, so to speak, this looks like a spur-of-the-moment killing. Is that right?"

"It—looks that way," said Frank, not sure, without Don's guidance, how much he was supposed to say about such matters.

"In which case," she continued, "I can only assume it's an argument that went too far." She blushed suddenly, and slapped herself on the thigh with her gardening gloves. "But I daresay a team of specially-trained detectives working around the clock has already arrived at that startling insight. Silly cow, keep your mouth shut!"

"No, not at all," said Frank. "It's an interesting point. Be even more interesting if you could—"

"If I could suggest who Beans might have been arguing with. Yes, I know, that's why it was daft of me to mention it. Because there wasn't anyone really."

"No one at all?"

"Well, nothing serious. And nothing you don't know about, I'm sure."

"Assume we know nothing," said Frank. He dropped his voice and added, "You wouldn't be that far off the mark, to tell you the truth."

Queer Gear laughed. "All right. Well, Beans hadn't been very happy with the Addams Family and that awful Mr. Perfect, lately. Neither of them was sufficiently anti the development scheme for his liking. Or for mine, come to that."

She paused, thinking, and Frank said, "Nobody

else?'' at just the same moment as she said, ''And of course—oh, sorry.''

''No, no,'' said Frank. ''Please go on.''

''I was only going to say there was that running argument—if you could call it that, it wasn't really that serious—with Joe and Dill, about Plot 14. Though it's very hard to imagine that coming to blows, let alone fatal force.''

''How do you mean?'' said Frank. ''Joe and Dill?''

Picking up on his suddenly heightened interest, she frowned. Both of them looked over at Don, and then looked at each other again. ''Surely you've heard about that? Beans and Dill—the American woman, yes?—were badgering Compost Joe to swap plots with them.''

''Beans, yes; Joe told us about that himself. But Dill—are you sure? Absolutely sure?''

She nodded. ''Sure I'm sure. Joe told me himself. He made a joke of it, you know—*Suddenly I'm Mr. Popularity,* sort of thing. Why, do you think it could be significant?''

He grinned. ''I hope so. Heaven knows, something's got to be, sooner or later.''

''YOU'VE REALLY GOT IT in for me, haven't you?'' said Compost Joe, speaking to Frank, but with his eyes straying to Don, who loitered on the path.

He probably thinks this is some good cop/bad cop performance, thought Frank. ''We've got it in for no one,'' he said. ''Least of all you, Joe, after all the help you've given us already.''

''Well, then,'' Joe grumbled. ''Not my fault you couldn't prove anything against Mr. Perfect, is it?''

"Absolutely not, Joe. No one's saying it is. No, this is something else that's come up, which we hope you can help us with again."

"What's it about, then?"

"We know that Beans was after you to swap plots, and we were just—"

"Of course you know that! I bloody told you that! Honestly, you're not seriously suggesting I killed poor old Beans just to stop him nagging me to swap plots, are you? Bloody hell, you really are scraping the bottom of the proverbial, you are."

More than you know, thought Frank. "I'm not suggesting that for a moment, Joe. It's just that we have to check and double check everything. You're a scientist, you understand that. You of all people."

"Yeah, well..."

"Thanks," said Frank. "Now, you said Beans was eager to get hold of your allotment, yes?"

Joe flared up again. He wouldn't easily forgive the police officers for seeing him in his home environment, Frank realised. "That's hardly a motive for murder, is it? Anyway, I *told* you all that."

"You did," Frank agreed. "But you didn't tell us that Dill had also been after your plot."

Joe was quiet for a moment. Then, with an irritated frown, he said, "Who told you that?"

"Someone mentioned it," Frank replied. "That both Dill and Beans had been badgering you to get you to swap plots."

"Oh, right!" said Joe, and Frank was sure he saw relief on his face. "Yeah, yeah, I remember. No, listen, I wasn't keeping anything from you. I just forgot, that's all."

"You forgot?"

"Sure. Why not? It wasn't relevant to what you were asking, was it? Anyway, she only asked once or twice, and that was a few weeks back, and she was perfectly polite about it. The thing is, when Beans started on it, he was going on and on about it, so that stuck in my mind. It got on my tits a bit, tell you the truth. Whereas Dill, she just mentioned it in passing. Almost jokingly, really. And when I made it clear I wasn't interested, she just let it drop."

"I see." Frank just hoped Don was taking all this in, at some subconscious level. Because it was more than his untrained detective's mind could process on its own. "Why did she want the plot, did she say?"

"Better drainage, she reckoned. For her herbs. See, the soil here is basically clay, quite heavy, quite damp. You understand?"

Frank nodded. Back on his own subject, Joe was becoming animated again, almost friendly.

"You can't dig too deep, not if you haven't got the organic matter in the topsoil, because all you'll do is bring up solid clay. And you can't rotovate, because with all the couch grass we've got here, that'd just cover the whole place with weeds. Therefore, it's basically a matter of building up the soil fertility from above—compost, green manures, etcetera. But if you look at Dill's plot—" He and Frank did so. "You'll see it's in a very slight valley, which of course makes it that much boggier. Whereas mine, you see, is atop a slight rise, which gives it better drainage."

"Right."

"Which is what you need for herbs," said Joe.

"Which, as you know, is what Dill grows. For her daft potions."

"OK." Frank jotted some notes that he hoped would make sense later. "So why wouldn't you swap? Make her happy, do you no harm. Or don't you want to get on her right side?" he added with what he hoped was a lads-together cheeky grin.

Joe shrugged. "She's not bad looking for her age, I suppose. But no, seriously, I just don't believe in it. You should go for your double, I reckon."

"Go for your...?"

"You know," said Joe. "Deal the hand you're dealt."

"I see what you mean," said Frank. And he did, though he wasn't convinced bloody-mindedness was something to be so proud of.

"DILL NEXT, THEN?"

Don didn't even shrug. Frank felt about ready to cry; uniformed constables were not supposed to run murder inquiries on their own. Not even murder inquiries which weren't going anywhere.

"I mean, she's the only one we've had any new info on for ages, isn't she? Petty as it is."

This time, Don shrugged. Was that progress?

Frank swore, shook his head in anger, and started off towards Dill's plot.

"No, wait," said Don.

"Oh, you still with us, are you, sir?" Frank couldn't resist the dig, though it didn't make him feel any better.

"I'm thinking, that's all, Frank," said Don. "You're doing fine, but I don't want to do Dill here.

I want to have an excuse for another poke round her house. Meet you there tonight at 8.30. All right?''

Relief battled with anger in Frank's mind; relief at having the burden of the investigation lifted from his shoulders…and anger at having the burden of the investigation lifted from his shoulders. ''Right, sir. Finished for now, are we?''

''No,'' said Don. ''We'll do the last two here. Starting with Squirrel.''

Their luck was in, as they found Squirrel and Tropical together, on one of Squirrel's plots which bordered Tropical's realm. The two men were clearly having an important conversation.

''That's interesting,'' said Frank. ''I didn't get the impression Squirrel was the sociable sort.''

As they got nearer, it became clear that the two plotters were not engaging in social chat, but in a decently restrained, not entirely unfriendly argument. About slug pellets, apparently.

''The thing is, friend,'' said Tropical, ''you know I have this wildlife pool on my plot.''

''Yes, yes—''

''And I'm afraid your pellets will poison the frogs and the hedgehogs that—''

''They won't.'' Squirrel shook his head. ''They're the mollusc-specific kind. They're safe for pets, children—''

''I know, I know,'' Tropical interrupted. ''But you're forgetting the food chains, right? OK, so the pellet itself doesn't poison the frog, but then the frog eats the dead slug, and—''

''Ah-ha!'' said Squirrel, raising a finger to score a point. ''But if, as you organic lot claim, amphibians are such great slug-hunters, then what's it doing eating *dead* slugs in the first place? Hey? What's it doing eating *dead* slugs?''

Eavesdropping from the path, unnoticed by either combatant, Frank was amazed at how animated Squirrel seemed—despite the fact that he was talking gardening, instead of doing it. Their discussion had much of the theological about it, and both men seemed to be enjoying it; yet it was clearly, also, a matter of profoundly passionate importance to them both. For the first time, really, Frank began to think maybe Don was right: there could be motives for murder on this site, which would seem trivial only to those who weren't involved.

''OK,'' said Tropical. ''Forget poisoning. What are the slug-eating animals supposed to live on if there's no slugs to eat? If all the slugs have been wiped out by your pellets?''

''Wait a minute,'' said Squirrel, his voice rising on the last syllable. ''Wait a *minute!* You're telling me I can't use slug pellets because they get rid of slugs? That's absolutely—''

''I'm not *telling* you anything, friend,'' Tropical insisted. ''I am merely suggesting, why not try a longer-term solution to the problem. When have you ever heard me complain of a slug problem on my plot? Never, right? And that's because I deliberately attract wildlife, which—''

''But if you've got no problem,'' crowed Squirrel, ''then what is your problem?''

''Because, now that you are using pellets along the border here, now I will have a problem. Listen, just try it and I guarantee you will soon see—''

Time to talk, Frank thought, and Don obviously wasn't going to make the first move. He might have recovered from an hour ago, but he still wasn't fully human.

"You're not an organics man yourself then, Mr. Wilson?" said Frank, stepping on to the plot. Both men looked at him, and behind him at Don, and both gave self-conscious laughs.

"I am not. I leave that to the hobby gardeners," Squirrel replied, a stiff smile not entirely drawing the sting from his words. Frank wondered what on earth he thought he was, if not a hobby gardener.

With a nod at Tropical, Squirrel went about his business. Frank let him go; he'd talk to Tropical first.

He looked over at Don, but the DI just shook his head, quickly, which Frank took as an instruction that he should lead the interview.

Interview? What did he have, to put to this man? The notional motive they had agreed on for Tropical was the obvious one—that Beans had shown him some kind of racialist hostility. And, yes, Frank could imagine that the man standing, smiling before him might rise to anger under such provocation. Could imagine him killing. But above all, he could imagine him keeping secrets. Looking at him now, he could quite believe that he would take more secrets to his grave than most people took teeth.

No, if there was anything to come out about Tropical, he was quite sure, it would come out by accident, by serendipity, not by interrogation.

Still…he had to say something. If only for the sake of face.

At that moment, however, Squirrel wheeled a full

barrow along the path, asked Don to "Mind his back," and Don saved Frank from having to say anything, by putting a hand, more affectionate than arresting, on Squirrel's shoulder, and asking Tropical, "What do you reckon, Jaime? Obviously this bloke's a nut, but is he nutty enough to kill?"

The distaste with which Tropical greeted the intervention was written on his face as he replied. "Anyone can kill, Inspector."

"Of course," said Don, "but—"

"No," said Tropical, and silence fell. "You policemen may think you know that. But me, I *know* it." He blinked, as if to remember where he was, and continued more softly. "However, ask yourself this: is my friend here organised enough to kill, and then to stay silent?"

"How do you mean, Jaime?" asked Frank.

"I mean, is this not puzzling? That the killing of poor Beans appears to have been a crime of passion. And yet the murderer—presumably a one-time only killer, not intending to kill, distraught at having done so—has managed to remain undetected."

"That sounds like you're volunteering, Jaime," said Don. "Anything you'd like to tell us?"

Squirrel, clearly irritated at the DI's condescending treatment, shook himself free of Don's arm and said, "You should ask me the same question. And I'll tell you the obvious: that Jaime couldn't even kill slugs, so how could he kill a human being?"

Frank felt Squirrel's intervention was intended more as a jibe at his fellow plotter, than as a character reference.

"Not sure that's the same thing," said Don.

"Surely even Jaime would kill slugs if his life depended on it."

But Squirrel was adamant. "No, I don't believe gardeners are made of the right stuff for murder, Inspector. They may lose their tempers, of course, that can happen to anyone. But as Jaime says, they wouldn't be able to follow through, they wouldn't be able to cover up their crimes."

"Perhaps," Don began, but Squirrel hadn't finished.

"You're interviewing the wrong people," he said. "You should be talking to the non-gardeners."

Frank was puzzled. Didn't everyone on the site know by now that the killer was definitely one of them? "Who do you mean," he asked. "Non-gardeners?"

"I mean those who rent allotments but have no real interest in gardening."

"I'm afraid we've already been down that road," said Frank, thinking of Mr. Perfect—still the only one with what he considered a half-way decent motive. Even so, something about Squirrel's logic struck a chord somewhere, and he noted the remark in his notebook for later perusal.

EIGHTEEN

AT FIRST, when Don rapped a perfunctory key on his car window outside Dill's house that night, and Frank looked out at the DI's blank face, he thought: "Hello, Don's Down."

But then, as he got out of the car and they exchanged good evenings, he began to think that Don wasn't Down, after all: just tired and low, presumably because the case was going nowhere. Interesting, Frank thought—even depressives can get depressed.

They leaned against Frank's car for a while, talking in low voices about the coming interview. "No real reason to reckon she's a better bet than any of the others, is there?" said Frank, feeling about as disconsolate as Don looked. Going home and then coming back to work, that was a special type of torture. It reminded him of junior school, when he'd only lived round the corner so he'd had his lunches at home, and then had to kiss his Ma goodbye for a second time every day before returning to face the afternoon's imprisonment.

"No real reason, no," Don agreed. "Except for the obvious."

"What obvious?"

"That we haven't really put her under any pressure

yet; that we don't really fancy any of the others; and that, for fuck's sake, it has to be one of them!''

DILL WAS NOT PLEASED to see them. She made a point of standing solidly in her doorway, so that they had to actually ask to come in. "I saw you asking questions around the allotments today, Inspector," she said as they stood in her living room (they had not yet been invited to sit). "Why didn't you speak to me then, instead of coming round here at this time of night, disturbing my evening?"

Don looked at her for a moment, smiling. Then he sat down, swung one leg over the other like a man at home, and said, "Sorry about that, madam. My constable had a headache. But we're here now."

Now she looked at him, as he'd looked at her. Like the Tyson/Bruno weigh-in, Frank thought. He hadn't bet on that fight—you could take patriotism too far, he reckoned—and he wouldn't bet on this one. Leonora Daniels maybe had the weight, the reach and the punch. But could she fight dirty like Don Packham?

She turned towards Frank and said, very pointedly, "Would you care for a seat, Constable?"

"Thank you, Ms. Daniels," he replied.

"Can I offer you a cup of tea?" she asked, still with her back to Don.

"That'd be lovely," said Don. "Herbal, preferably. Camomile or tansy or peppermint…?"

Still without facing him, she replied, "I have PG Tips."

"Even more preferable," said Don. "After all, all tea's herbal, isn't it? What's tea if it's not a herb?"

As soon as she was out of the room, Don was out

of his seat. Frank was relieved to see that, without a search warrant, he wasn't opening drawers or moving papers. Indeed, he very properly kept his hands in his pockets as he stuck his nose into Dill's bookcases, bureaux, occasional tables and the like.

"Lots of business stuff," Don whispered, jerking his chin at piles of account books, stationery, and similar paraphernalia.

"Yeah," Frank whispered back. "But no books on gardening. Nothing about herbs." He was thinking of what Squirrel had said, that afternoon. Look for the non-gardeners. "Suppose Beans found out something about her life back in the States?"

"Like what?"

Frank shrugged, as quietly as he could. "Maybe her herbal potions hurt someone?"

"Talking about me, boys?" said Dill, coming back into the room carrying a tea tray. Cake as well as PG Tips, Frank noted; and a forced laugh in her voice. She's decided to be nice after all. Wonder why?

Don, it soon became clear, had not decided to be nice. "Our best guess at the moment, Ms. Daniels," he said, his tea and cake untouched, "is that you murdered Beans because he wouldn't let you take over leadership of the Allotment Society."

She laughed, and this time Frank felt the laugh wasn't forced. Or was less forced, at any rate. "That's your best guess, Inspector? Oh my God, you poor guys. Can you imagine a jury... Oh dear, forgive me, but I haven't had a lot to laugh about lately."

"You're overdoing it," said Don. "A simple 'Are you out of your mind, officer' would have sufficed."

"No. No, I don't think it would. You see, one of

the things I like best about this country is the way you people laugh at yourselves. And I am asking you just for a moment to consider how enormously amusing the English, of all people, would find the idea that you have just put to me. I mean, it's like the plot of some hokey British movie, you know? Starring Hugh Grant, or something. Honestly, Inspector!''

"So what you're saying, Ms. Daniels, is that no jury would swallow it. You're not saying, I notice, that it's not the truth.''

She sighed, took a sip of tea. Sighed again, and leant forward to look right into Don's eyes. ''I did not kill Beans,'' she said. ''And I can promise you, whoever did kill him, did not do so in order to wrest control of the People's Republic of Crockett's Drive! It's just not that sort of deal, Inspector. You've obviously never done much voluntary work, or you'd know—people kill each other to *avoid* getting elected chairman.''

Don drank half his cup of tea in one swallow, as if refreshing himself, Frank fancied, at the sound of the bell. ''Very well, then,'' said Don. ''If you didn't kill him because of the Allotment Society, then I suppose you must have killed him because he was blackmailing you.''

Frank couldn't be certain, but it seemed to him perhaps that Dill's stillness was more than natural. ''Blackmailing?'' she said. ''I don't believe Beans was a blackmailer. Do you have evidence that he was a blackmailer?''

''Whereabouts in America do you come from, by the way?''

She blinked. ''What?''

"Where did you live in America, Ms. Daniels?"

"I—all over the place. I moved around a lot."

"Sure," said Don. "But most recently, before you came to this country?"

"Chicago," she said. And blinked again.

"Cold."

"So's England."

"Right," said Don, standing swiftly, and rubbing his hands together. For a white-facing moment, Frank thought he was going to arrest her. "Thanks for the tea."

"You're—" She shook her head, as if to clear it, and stood up. "That's it? You're going?"

"That's all," Don smiled. "For the moment."

As soon as she'd shut the front door behind them, Don punched Frank on the arm and said, "Rattled her, eh? Definitely rattled her!"

"Well, yeah," said Frank, unlocking his car door. "But the way you went at her would have rattled an innocent person just as much as a guilty one. Maybe more."

"No, she's the one, Frank. She is the one." They got into Frank's car, and the DI lit a cigar.

"So now we're saying Beans *was* a blackmailer?" said Frank.

"I don't know, maybe. Or maybe they did fall out over the Allotment Society business, and he just wanted to get back at her. Either way, he's found out something about her, and she's topped him for it. Take my word for it. Better yet, don't take my word for it—you're friendly with that Lucy girl at the station, aren't you?" He handed Frank his mobile phone. "Sweet talk her into tickling that computer for us."

By NINE the next morning, Lucy and her computer were in receipt of the information that no Leonora Daniels, matching the parameters provided, was known to the FBI.

"You can't prove a negative," Don insisted. "Tell Lucy to let her imagination run free."

"How do you mean?" asked Frank.

"Just let her loose on the computer, and see what she can come up with from anywhere. Any and all information concerning Dill gratefully received. After all, there's no reason why whatever it is she's hiding should be something that happened in the USA."

At six that evening ("Don't bother putting in for overtime," Don told Frank. "CID hours have to be a little more flexible than what you're used to") Lucy reported that, as far as she had been able to discover, Leonora Daniels hadn't existed until eighteen months ago, when she rented the allotment, and the house where she currently lived.

"Rented?" said Frank. "I thought she owned it."

Don nodded. "Rich widow, right? So why is she throwing her money away on rent? And in any case, why give the impression that she owned the place?"

"If she's only been around eighteen months," said Frank, "then we're back to looking for skeletons in her American closet, yeah? But the problem with that is, and always has been, how would Beans know about it? His specialty was local history, not US history. He's never been to America, as far as we know."

"Check that," said Don. "The point is, she is living under a false name."

"Not necessarily. If she's only been in the country eighteen months—"

"No," said Don. "One of the checks Lucy did was with immigration. There's no record of Leonora Daniels entering the country—not under that name."

"OK. But you can call yourself what you want, can't you? So there's no crime."

"Doesn't matter," said Don. "She has lied to us about who she is whilst knowing that she was a suspect in a murder inquiry. Now, if she won't tell us her real name when we directly ask her for it—well, if that doesn't count as suspicious behaviour, I don't know what would."

"Certainly gives us grounds to re-interview her," Frank agreed.

"Bloody right it does. She's the one, Frank. She killed him."

"WE HAVE REASON to believe," Don said, shouldering past Dill into her house, almost before she'd finished opening the door, "that you have lied to us during the course of a murder investigation. We are here now to get the truth." Spotting the phone standing on a table in the hall, he picked up the receiver and handed it to her. "Want to call a lawyer?"

"Would you care to come in?" She sounded sharper than she looked, Don thought. She knew what this was about, all right.

"Don't mess us around any more, I'm warning you. You have given us a false name, and I am quite sure you understand just how suspicious that looks to a policeman investigating a murder."

She took the phone from him, and slammed it back on its cradle. "Not at all, Inspector, your amateur dramatics notwithstanding. I adopted the name Leonora Daniels when I came to Cowden. For my own reasons.

Personal reasons. And that makes it my name—you can call yourself anything you want in this country, you know. That's the law.'' Now she pushed past him, and strode into the living room.

Instead of following, Don raised his voice to cover the extra distance. See how she likes having a shouting detective in her hallway, he thought. See just how suburban she really is. ''Broadly speaking, that is so. However, the law on names is a deal more complicated than most people imagine,'' he said, having no idea whether that was true or not. ''I daresay that if we looked hard enough we could find some law you've broken, by giving a false name. And I am entirely confident that, under the circumstances, I could get a warrant to search this place.'' He softened his voice. ''Having a dozen stonefaced young coppers combing through your possessions isn't a very pleasant experience even if you're guilty, believe me. And if you're innocent...''

''I am innocent,'' she said.

''But you're still not going to tell us your real name?''

She, too, seemed to make an effort to soften her voice, and her face. She even tried a small, crooked smile. ''Look, Inspector, I am innocent. And, yes, I do understand how this must look to you. I'm sorry I snapped at you—you're only doing your job, I know. It's just that I really value my privacy. I've made a new start here in London, a new life, and this is all part of it.''

''So?'' Don prompted.

''So... Yes, I will tell you my name. My old name. But first, like you said, I think I should talk to a lawyer. I am an American, after all.'' Don moved to pick up the phone again, but Dill said, "No, in private. When I've spoken to the lawyer, I'll call you. I promise."

Could he take her in, Don wondered. Did he have anything that would work against her? No, better this way. She had to give them the name sooner or later, surely.

"OK. But don't bother phoning. Instead, I want you to report in person to me at Cowden police station, within the next twenty-four hours, with a passport or birth certificate or some other official document made out in your original name. Otherwise I'll be back with that search warrant. Do you understand?"

She sighed, and smiled again, her shoulders loosening with relief. "Thank you, Inspector. Yes, I understand."

AT TWO O'CLOCK the next morning, Don was woken by a call from the duty sergeant at Cowden nick. Three hours earlier, a woman had attempted to board a flight to Spain at Heathrow airport, using a Canadian passport in the name of Moira McLennan. A security officer, observing her nervous manner, had asked if he might look in her bag. There he had found other documents in the name of Leonora Daniels. The woman had been unable to provide any reasonable explanation of this discrepancy, and the security officer had therefore held her in custody while he checked with the police station nearest to the address on the Leonora Daniels documentation, to find out if she was known to them.

She was, and Moira McLennan was currently in a cell at Cowden police station. Would Don like a word with her?

NINETEEN

"HELLO?" SHE LOOKED AT the digital clock: 2:09.

"That'd be Debbie, would it?"

"Who is this, please?" Debbie asked—although, later, she realised she'd known who it was even before she'd picked up the phone.

"My name's Don Packham. We've not met, Debbie—and I do apologise for choosing such an absurdly early hour of the morning at which to introduce myself."

"Not at all, Mr. Packham," she murmured, her mouth still full of nocturnal sludge. "Very nice to meet you. Would you care for a fairy cake?"

She held the phone away from her ear as Don's delighted laugh boomed down the line. "Oh, you are lovely, Mrs. Mitchell. Don't fancy an affair, I suppose?"

"Not at such an absurdly hour of the earling, thank you, no," she mumbled, digging Frank in the side and ribs with an elbow and hip. He could sleep through anything, jammy bugger. As her husband at last opened his eyes, she gave him a thumb's up sign. He looked at her blankly.

"Fair enough, Debbie," Don chortled. "I'll let you get back to sleep if you'll just give me a word with the constable."

Frank took the phone. "Hello?...Oh, yes sir....No, not at all, Don, no problem...No, no, we were just...well, we were just asleep, actually...What, now?...No, great idea, I just wonder if this isn't something that might better be done by daylight..." He grimaced at Debbie, but received no solidarity from her, as she was asleep again, her head on his stomach. "You'll tell me on the way...Fair enough. Yeah, thirty minutes, fine."

Frank hung up the phone. "Bastard," he said, and went straight back to sleep.

TWENTY-FIVE MINUTES LATER, the phone rang again. This time, Frank awoke instantly. He looked at the clock. "Oh fucking hell," he said.

He jumped out of bed and looked out of the window. Sure enough, as he'd feared, there was Don's car, and there was Don waving at him through the windscreen with one hand, while holding his mobile phone in the other.

DON, AS WAS HIS CUSTOM, said little during the drive to Beans's flat. Once they'd arrived, he told Frank why they were there.

"You see, Frank, this is good news for us, this airport arrest, but it's not the end of the world for her. Immigration had enough to hold her, and good enough reason to hand her over to us for first go. But now we've got to arrest her. You understand that? She's done nothing, as far as we know, that's going to get her put away."

"Except murder," said Frank. Like all coppers he believed in the first rule of evidence: if you run, you're guilty. No further proof needed, except by over-cautious courts.

"Right," said Don. "At the moment, what have we got? Some mix up over false names—if there's no criminal deception involved, then it's nothing. So when we go in and interview her, the clock is going to be ticking away. We have got to have something more than we've got now that makes her look like a murderer. Understood?"

"Understood."

"Or even something that makes her *smell* like a murderer. This is penalty shoot-out time, Frank. We get one chance, and then we've lost her."

"So what exactly are we looking for here?"

"Still the same as before," said Don. "Something, anything, that provides a link between Dill and Beans, other than the fact that they just happen to be neighbours on the allotments. The difference is, this time, we have a little more to go on."

"We know her name," agreed Frank. "Moira McLennan."

They let themselves into Beans's flat as quietly as possible. They didn't want Miss Leicher or any other vigilant, insomniac neighbour, reporting them to the police as burglars—not because they didn't have every right to be there, but because the humour which such a situation would give rise to back at the station would be of long duration, and entirely at their expense.

The search itself was something of an anti-climax.

Three of the volumes in Beans's modest library were published by the Cowden Press—a semi-amateur outfit, Don guessed, with an address at the other end of the borough. The books dealt with various aspects of Cowden life in the first half of the twentieth century, making great use of old photographs and local newspaper archives. The individual titles in the series were: Transport, War, and Crime.

In the index to the Crime volume, the name "McLennan" appeared; not as part of the printed index, but inserted, in what Don assumed was Beans's handwriting. He'd half noticed it before, idly flicking through the pages of the book to see if anything was concealed between its leaves. But then, of course, the name had meant nothing to him.

"What do you make of that, Frank?" he passed the book over to the constable.

"Bloody hell. That's Dill's name."

"Name on her passport, anyway," said Don. "Looks like an amendment, doesn't it? As if he was correcting an omission made by the author."

"SORRY TO KEEP YOU so long, Moira," Don told her, once the tape recorder was running in the interview room. "But I've been rather busy since you arrived here."

Dill looked at him with cool eyes, and said nothing.

"What I've been doing, in fact, is getting the paperwork sorted out which will allow me to dig up plot Number 14 on the Crockett's Hill Allotment Site."

The DI was lying, Frank knew—playing a hunch, bluffing. On the way back to the nick, they had discussed once again the relationship between Dill and Beans, as far as they knew it.

"We're going to dig up Compost Joe's plot," Don said. "The one you and Beans were so keen to get hold of. Care to tell us now what it is we're looking for?"

Still she didn't speak.

"You tried to flee the country when we found out that you were using a false name, Moira," Don went on. "That on its own, I believe, gives us enough to hold you while our inquiries continue. I'll be speaking to the Chief Superintendent about that shortly, in fact."

Her surrender, when it came, seemed as total as it was sudden. But Frank, taking the role of observer in this session by prearrangement, was sure that just before her face collapsed, and she started crying and then talking, he had seen a look of pure calculation cross her features. She was going to tell them the story now, he thought, but she was going to tell it in a way designed to put her in as sympathetic a light as possible.

She was speaking for the tape; well, you could hardly blame her for that.

"My name was Moira McLennan," she began, "before I came back to Cowden."

"*Back* to Cowden?" said Don.

"I have lived most of my life in Canada. No, not the United States, Inspector—that was, well, sort of a lie." She smiled and wiped her eyes with a tissue. "I was born here, locally, the illegitimate and initially unacknowledged daughter of a man named Peter McLennan. My mother gave me his name."

"But you didn't live with him?"

As if ignoring the question, Dill continued, "When I was seven years old, I emigrated to Canada. With my mother and father." She paused, and her eyes invited Don to ask the obvious question.

"With your mother and father? So. What happened to his wife?"

"I think you already know the answer to that, Inspector. I didn't, of course. Not then. I always knew my parents weren't married, though that was a family secret, it wasn't something you shouted about in respectable Canada in those days. But I was told that my father's wife had left him, because they didn't love each other like he and Mom did. Left him, just before we left England."

"And when did you learn different?"

"My father made what I'm afraid can only be described as a death-bed confession. He had cancer, and one day very near the end he told me that he had killed his wife. Killed her because he loved me and he loved Mom and she wouldn't divorce him, and he couldn't bear to live without us. So he killed her, and buried her on his allotment."

"Plot Number 14 on Crockett's Drive?" said Don. Dill nodded.

"Why do you think he told you?" Don asked. "After all those years. Why burden you with it?"

"Confession," she said, without hesitation. "He was a lapsed Catholic—but not so lapsed that he could go to his maker without unburdening himself. At least, that was what I thought at first. Now I think maybe he just wanted to burden me with it."

"Why should he do that?"

"Because he blamed me for the way his life had turned out. My parents' marriage, so-called, was not a happy one."

"What was your reaction to this confession?"

"I was touched. Horrified. Afraid." She shrugged.

"Exactly what you'd expect me to be. And I promised him that it would be our secret, that I would never breathe a word of it to Mom, never burden her conscience with what had lain so heavily on his." She paused, rubbed her eyes. Bet she wishes these interviews were video'd, thought Frank.

"And?" said Don. "What was his reaction to that?"

"He laughed," said Dill, laughing herself, fresh tears coming to her eyes. "The last time I ever heard my father laugh. And he said—Your mother knows, girly. Your mother helped me bury her."

"An awful shock for you, Moira," said Don. "Did you discuss this with your mother?"

"No. No, never. Even though I believed what he'd told me—the way he said it, I just knew it was true— I was sure that anything Mom had done had been under duress. I don't mean necessarily he forced her, but...well, Inspector, a woman in love will do all sorts of crazy things."

"Then what brought you back to England?"

"I had a plan. My Mom is a good woman. A Christian woman. I could only guess at the torture she must have gone through all those years, waiting for someone to discover the body on Plot 14, waiting for the authorities to track her and my father down. Waiting for it all to come out, all the shame and tragedy and, presumably, prison."

"But you had a plan to release her from this torture?"

"That's right. I've never married, Inspector—that was another untruth, I'm afraid. I had a good career, and I—"

"What sort of career?" Don interrupted.

"Oh, just, you know—business. Anyway, the point is, I had money saved. So I gave up my job, told Mom I'd got a great offer to work in London for a couple of years. And I hopped on a plane for Heathrow. Day after my father's funeral. Came home to Cowden."

"As Leonora Daniels," said Don.

"As a stranger, right. I hoped to find the allotments built on—but, as you know, they were still there, still being cultivated. So I rented one. Had to go on a waiting list for two months—that was torture, if you like—and even then I couldn't get my father's old plot."

"What was the point of taking an allotment? What did you plan to do?"

"Simply, Inspector, to retrieve the body, dispose of it somewhere more permanent. And then fly home to Mom, and tell her that she didn't need to be afraid anymore. We could live out the rest of our lives together in something approaching peace."

How were you going to move the body, thought Frank. Hire a bulldozer?

"How on earth were you going to move the body, Moira?" Don asked.

She shook her head impatiently. "Look, I'm not pretending this was a rational plan, OK? This was something crazy, I see that now, done from love. From fear. I think maybe I did go a little crazy after Daddy died. Wouldn't you?"

If Don was irritated by her theatrics, he didn't show it. Mildly, he pushed the story on. "And then you found out about the land deal. That must have come as a nasty shock."

"Oh sweet Jesus, did it ever! Suddenly, I was working against the clock. I had to delay the development plans as long as possible, at the same time finding a way to gain access to Plot 14 before the earth-movers moved in. You see, the chances of anyone digging up the body through ordinary gardening were pretty remote. If you dig deep on that kind of clay soil, you just bring up more clay, so most of the cultivation is done by adding organic matter to the surface. So, in effect, the body of my father's wife was getting buried deeper every year. But putting up a block of offices—well, that's a different matter."

"All right," said Don. "I see your predicament. So where does Beans come into all this?"

"Beans." She rubbed her hands across her eyes, making them redder than ever. "That was my idea, you know? All those stupid nicknames. All the better to preserve my anonymity, I thought. I needn't have bothered. Arthur Jones was suspicious of me, I believe, almost from the beginning. Almost from the day I arrived."

"How come? Your cover story was pretty convincing, I would have thought."

"Truth is, I reckon he was suspicious way back when it all happened. You know he had an allotment there even then? So he knew my father, before we emigrated. The story my parents put around then, according to my father's last confession, was pretty much the same one they'd always told me: that his wife went back to her people in Ireland when she found out about him having an affair. She had no family in England, not many friends."

"But you think Arthur had his suspicions even then?"

"I get the impression—I don't know, I think maybe he just didn't like my father. Knowing Beans, he probably disapproved of his mulching methods or something. And I don't doubt he disapproved of him upping and leaving like that, without tendering the proper period of notice to the Allotment Society. You know, the kind of guy he is? So maybe he would have had suspicions based on prejudice, and just by coincidence they happened to be right."

"So he was suspicious of your father, and the circumstances in which he left England. But why should he be suspicious of you, all those years later?"

She twisted her mouth into a wry smile. "Despite my accent, my age, my invented life history, all my attempts at camouflage—you know what? I'm the spitting image of my father. Ain't that something, Inspector? I look just like my old man. I think all that business had been fermenting away in Arthur Jones's tiny little brain all those years, and then as soon as he saw me, wham! It all clicked into place."

"OK," said Don. "But couldn't you have just kept out of his way?"

"No, no, don't you see? Because of the development threat hanging over the site, and because he was nominally the chairman of the Allotment Society, I had to talk to him all the time. You were right about that, incidentally—me and old Beans, we were rivals for leadership of the tenants. For him it was pride, stubbornness, macho shit. But for me—for me, it was life or death! He was so useless, he never could have delayed the development, let alone stopped it. I had to take over from him. I had to!"

"And meanwhile, you were trying to get hold of Plot 14."

"Yeah—and that fruitcake compost man wouldn't give it up. What is it with you British men and your damn territorial instinct? Like a load of kids, I'm not kidding. Or dogs. Anyway, as soon as Beans heard I was after Joe's plot—guess what? He's after it, too. I tell you, Inspector, I was getting frantic. I'd come here on a mission of mercy. OK, a crazy mission, maybe, but that's all it was. And now, I was in danger of making things *worse* for my Mom. Attracting attention to Plot 14 and what's buried there. Giving the cops new clues as to what had happened, and where to look for the culprits. I was on the verge of cutting and running, and that's the truth."

"Had Beans actually said anything to you? I mean, said anything right out?"

Dill straightened her shoulders, and put her hands one on top of the other on the table. Her voice when she spoke again was quiet and sad. "No. Just hints. Until the Sunday before last."

"The day he died?"

"That's right, Inspector. The day I killed him."

Would the tape pick up the deafening sound of two policemen holding their breath, Frank wondered?

"You killed Arthur Jones, a week ago yesterday?" said Don.

"I did," said Dill. "I went over to his plot to talk to him about some Society business. A petition we were getting up. But he wasn't interested. Well, that was nothing new; he was never interested in any of my ideas. Instead, he showed me a page from one of his damn local history scrapbooks. A page from a ring-binder, you know?''

"And what was on this page?'' asked Don, careful not to put words in her mouth.

"It was a Xerox of an old local newspaper. He got it from the library, I guess. From a month or so after we emigrated to Canada. The letters page.''

"A letter to the editor?'' said Don.

She nodded. "From a neighbour of my father's. A woman, an Irish name. I don't remember. I only saw it briefly before Beans snatched it back.''

"What was the letter about?''

"Does anybody know the whereabouts of Charity McLennan. I have property of hers, and am unable to trace her in Ireland.''

"So she did have a friend in England after all?''

"So it seems, Inspector. So it seems. And Beans was—he was taunting me with it, teasing me. I know who you are, he kept saying, and I know why you're here. I swear, Inspector, you've got to believe me, this wasn't a planned murder. Look, I know what I've done is crazy and terrible and—I killed him, and I accept responsibility for that, OK? But you've just got to believe me, it wasn't planned. It was almost an accident!''

"How did it happen?'' said Don.

She took in a long breath. "OK. He was waving this damn piece of paper at me, and I shoved him—you know, just shoved him away. I didn't realise how close we were to that bean trench, and he fell in. It was awful. I felt sick! It was the worst moment of my life!''

"Was he dead?''

"No." Dill was quiet again now, as she approached the climax of her tale. "He was badly injured. But he wasn't dead. And I panicked. I don't even remember doing it, to tell you the truth, but what I must have done is, picked up the fork and..." She trailed off, her sobs renewed. "It was an accident, Inspector! Almost, anyway—you do see that, don't you?"

"What did you do then, once he was dead?"

"Went back to my own plot, and waited for the body to be found. I didn't have to wait long."

They took her to the custody area, where she was charged with murder, and locked up.

DON WASN'T DOWN, exactly, Frank didn't think—but he wasn't ecstatic, either. Something was still bothering him.

"You do think she did it, don't you?" Frank asked, as they drank coffee in the canteen.

"Oh God yes, no doubt about that. It's just that..."

"Go on."

"There are always loose ends, Frank, it's true. But this one...OK. First of all, if it was a sudden, unplanned killing, like she says, why wasn't she in a state of shock when it was finished? Where did she learn to be so cool about killing another human being?" He began counting on his fingers. "Next, the picture she paints of Beans, a vicious, grudge-bearing, sadistic blackmailer. Does that sound like the Beans anyone else has told us about?"

"Not really," admitted Frank. After a moment, he added, "For what it's worth, something that bothered me."

"Yes?"

"Joe says she only made a token effort to get hold of his plot, the plot where her father's wife is supposedly buried. But from her account, she was desperate to get her hands on it."

"Bloody good point!" said Don. "And another thing, perhaps the biggest quibble of all. Why didn't she just leave well alone? She knew nothing about the land deal before she came here, and the body hadn't been discovered in all these years. So what were the chances of anyone finding it now? Or, indeed, of connecting it with her mother, an old widow living on the other side of the Atlantic?"

"And," said Frank, "even if it was connected to her father, all her mother's got to say is, Oh gosh how terrible, I never imagined him capable of such a thing. You'd have to be a genius to make a case against her that could stick." Frank's enthusiasm died as suddenly as it had flared. "But, Don, what are you saying? I mean, she did it, she's confessed to it, so—what, exactly?"

"Fair question." Don lit a cigar, in full view of three No Smoking signs, two Chief Inspectors and a Superintendent. "She did it, yes. And she's confessed to it. But she's confessed to a crime of passion. Basically, to manslaughter."

"Lighter sentence."

"Especially these days," said Don, his smile sour. "Women who kill men these days, they're more likely to get voted Heroine of the Year than they are to go to prison; you know that as well as I do."

Frank wasn't sure that was entirely true, but he didn't argue. "But you're saying it wasn't an argument gone wrong?"

"I'm bloody sure it wasn't, Frank. It doesn't fit Beans, and it doesn't fit Dill. No, she planned it, you can count on that. And as far as I can see, there's absolutely no way we could ever... Oh bloody hell!" he leapt to his feet. "We've missed something."

Frank followed as the DI ran back to the custody area. By the time Frank caught up, Don was already demanding the prisoner's possessions from the custody officer.

He dug around in Dill's shoulder bag, and pulled out her passport. "Here we are," he said. "Yes! I thought so. I saw it earlier on, but it didn't strike me then. Have a look at this, Frank."

Frank looked where Don pointed: the personal details page. For a long moment he wasn't sure what he was looking for.

And then he was. "Christ!" he said. "But—what does it mean?"

"I don't know, precisely," Don grinned. "But you've got to admit, she does look bloody good for her age, doesn't she?"

TWENTY

DON WAS DRESSED all in black. A dark, funereal suit which Frank hadn't seen before—and privately hoped never to see again; a black tie; a shirt of such a dark blue that it might as well have been black. Black shoes and socks.

He'd even had a haircut, in the hour or so since Frank had last seen him. A scalping, almost, the shortness of the remaining hair making it seem darker.

"You look ready for business, sir," Frank said.

"If I don't get her in this session, Frank, then she's not gettable. Simple as that." He ran his hands over his head, to flatten his already flat hair. He looked down at his toes, and breathed in, through his mouth, lung-bursting deep breaths, five of them in series, exhaled through the nose so slowly that Frank felt himself asphyxiating in sympathy.

"You all right?" he asked.

"Fine, Frank. I'm fine now. You OK with your part?"

Frank's part, as far as he knew, was to sit still and watch. He reckoned he could manage that. "Yes, no problem."

"Right then," said Don, straightening his back, and

stretching his facial muscles before the door to the interview room, as if before a full-length mirror. "Let's go in."

"HERE'S MY THEORY of what actually happened between you and Arthur Jones," said Don. His voice was quiet, calm, confident. But Moira McLennan's demeanour was all these things, too—and while Frank knew that Don was acting, he could only guess about Dill. "I think you killed him for profit. I think it was not the tragic near-accident which you described to us in your previous interview. Not the single moment of madness, of panic, of terror, that you would have us believe. But a premeditated, carefully planned and cunningly executed murder."

Two pairs of confident eyes stared at each other for a silent while. *For the benefit of the tape,* Frank thought, *neither blinked.*

"You have no comment to make, Ms. McLennan? No? Very well." Don glanced a question at Dill's lawyer, Kate Ferrold, a ferret-faced young woman with bad breath and a partnership in a City law firm which, it was rumoured, would make her a millionaire before she was thirty. She only accepted criminal cases, and only female clients. Don had little time for her.

The lawyer closed her eyes briefly. Too busy to actually shake her head, Frank supposed. He and Don were quite certain that Dill's decision to forgo representation during her first, tearful, confessional interview was every bit as calculated as her decision to have Kate Ferrold shield her now. The presence of such a woman could hardly help but unnerve an interrogator. Even without the bad breath.

"Very well," Don said again. "I believe that part of your plan concerning the murder of Arthur Jones, was to make his death look as if it were spur-of-the-moment. By so doing, you hoped to direct the attention of the police towards such motives as might be expected to lead to a violent argument—a disagreement over boundaries, perhaps, or slug pellets."

Shows how much she knows about plotters, thought Frank: they don't kill each other over their disagreements, they just nag each other to death.

"If, however," Don continued, "we, the investigating officers, were to conclude after all that the killing was pre-planned, then you were confident that we would soon turn our focus towards the proposed sell-off and development of the Crockett's Drive site. Indeed, you yourself did your best to steer us in that direction the very first time we spoke to you, on the day of Beans's death. Isn't that right, Constable Mitchell?"

Frank nodded. Or rather, he moved his jaw, once, in an affirmative manner. He was determined to match his opposite number, the silent, motionless lawyer, in both silence and motionlessness.

"The answer lies in the land, you told us," Don said. "Peasants being turfed off the soil by robber barons. You remember? But this plan of yours, Ms. McLennan, this plan for doing away with poor old Beans, was even more deeply plotted than that. This onion still had one more layer of peel to go."

He paused, but still the other three people in the room didn't move and didn't speak. Frank began to feel a yawn coming on: that always happened to him at tense moments, like job interviews and funerals. *Oh, God*, he prayed, please just let me die of a massive stroke before the yawn comes. I couldn't live, knowing that all this silent tape was punctured for posterity only by my yawn!

"You were not a professional killer, Ms. McLennan, and you knew your limitations. You knew that your knowledge of modern detective methods, of forensic science, of police procedures, was far from perfect. You knew, in other words, that despite all your best efforts, all your careful planning, you might still be caught. You might still be arrested. You might still end up here, with no alternative but confession."

Don reached behind him, to where a black briefcase lay on a spare chair. From it he withdrew a large manila envelope. He placed the envelope in front of him on the table, but made no immediate reference to it.

Frank checked: the lawyer was looking at it, the suspect wasn't. Well, well. And the yawn had gone. Thank God. Or did that mean he was about to die of a massive stroke?

"You approached this possibility coolly, logically, disinterestedly, as if it were a business problem," said Don. "Because that's what you are, isn't it? A cool, disinterested businesswoman. And the killing of Arthur Jones was, after all, merely a matter of business. And so you did what any sensible businesswoman would do, when she was planning any important risky piece of business. You prepared a final fall-back position, for if the very worst came to the very worst. Isn't that right, Ms. McLennan?"

Nothing. Not a flicker. The lawyer was staring at him now, Frank realised, presumably in an attempt to ruffle Frank, so that Frank in turn would distract Don. Well, he'd beaten the yawn. He could beat this, too.

No way was Frank Mitchell going to be the weak link here.

Don smiled and nodded at Dill, as if she'd answered his question. "That's right, Ms. McLennan. You prepared a motive for yourself, didn't you? For if you were arrested for the murder of Arthur Jones. If your attempt to leave the country on your real passport should for some reason, be frustrated. A soft motive. A motive based on a little girl's love for her Mommy. A motive based on a kind of crazy quest for justice. A very feminine motive, it must be said—not one that a man could ever hope to get away with. And this motive formed the basis of a story which, if told skilfully enough, by a female barrister to a male judge, would end up with you being almost more Arthur Jones's victim than he was yours."

Don picked up the manila envelope, slit its flap. And then put it down again, without looking inside. His theatrics worked, Frank saw: the lawyer's gaze jerked from Frank, to the envelope, to Don, and back to the envelope.

"Now, it may be," said Don, leaning back in his chair, linking his hands behind his head, "that you did indeed come back to Cowden with the intention of removing the body of your father's wife from Plot 14. Though I have to say that I find that rather difficult to believe. I wonder if, when we make inquiries of our colleagues in Canada, we will find that your picture of yourself as a lonely spinster devoted to her white-haired old mother will prove to be supportable. I wonder, indeed, whether we will even find that white-haired old mother still alive at all."

Dill smiled for the first time in the interview, and

Frank felt sure then that that part of her story, at least, would check out.

"I do know," Don continued, "that once you had decided that Beans had to die, you then approached your allotment neighbour, the man you called Compost Joe, and asked him to let you swap plots with him. And this presumably was done for two reasons: to prove to the police, should you ever need to, that you were desperate to gain access to Plot 14. And to provoke Arthur Jones into making a similar request to Joe. If this came out, it would look as if he was trying to beat you to the corpse. In fact, I suspect, he was merely angry at the thought of someone like you—not a proper allotmenteer at all, in his view—taking over such a prime plot."

Don picked up the envelope again. This time, he didn't put it down.

"Either way," he said, "you would have been very glad to have swapped allotments with Compost Joe, because his plot, Plot 14, really did offer better growing conditions for your herbs. And herbs, Ms. McLennan—that is what this is all about, isn't it?"

He opened the envelope, and took out a stapled batch of papers. "I am now showing the suspect some business papers recovered from her home in Cowden by a police search team earlier today. Do you recognise these papers, Ms. McLennan?"

No response, beyond a slightly puzzled frown on the lawyer's face. So, thought Frank, this is new to her, too.

"No?" said Don. "I'm surprised. I should have thought these papers would have been too important for you to have forgotten them. So let me remind you.

They are documents relating to a business deal which you are, evidently, on the verge of finalising with a national chain of stores, by the name of Natural Beauty. Now do you recall what we're talking about?''

Dill looked at her lawyer. The lawyer raised her eyebrows less than an inch. Dill cleared her throat. ''Yes, of course, Inspector. As you very well know, I have an interest in herbal cosmetics. Several of the preparations I have devised are, if all goes well, to be manufactured and marketed by Natural Beauty.''

''That's right,'' said Don. ''And you will, of course, be playing quite a part personally in the promotion of these preparations, won't you? As their devisor, and as your own human guinea pig.''

Not a flicker from Dill, although the lawyer, Frank noted, couldn't take her eyes off her client.

''Quite understandably so,'' said Don. ''Since, if you'll forgive me for saying so, you do look remarkably good for your age.'' He smiled at her, and then at her lawyer, whose expression of blatant bafflement caused both policemen considerable pleasure.

''You stand to make a very large amount of money from your little herbal potions, don't you, Ms. McLennan? And this, I suggest, lies at the root of your decision to murder Arthur Jones. You told us the truth when you said that you killed him because he had found out your secret. When you told us that he knew who you were—or who you had been, all those years previously. But I don't believe that he knew, or ever suspected, that your father's wife was buried on your father's old allotment. I don't think it ever crossed his mind. I think, rather, that the thing he knew about you, with all his fascination for, and unrivalled memory of, local history, was something far more potentially damaging to you, personally.''

Don opened the envelope again and this time withdrew a single sheet of paper. He pushed it across the table to Dill.

''I am showing the suspect a facsimile copy of her birth certificate.'' He leaned across to her, and said in a voice so soft that Frank wondered if the tape would pick it up: ''You are forty-five, Moira. Not fifty-five, as you claim. And as such, at the risk of sounding ungallant, I have to say that you don't look nearly so good for your age. Not to me…and not, I suspect, to the publicity department at Natural Beauty Ltd.''

FRANK AND DON drank their tea in the corridor, while Dill and her lawyer conferred in the interview room.

''One chance, you said,'' said Frank. ''Think we took it?''

''I don't know,'' said Don. ''I'd love to hear what her lawyer's saying to her right now. In the end, I think it probably depends on how well the details of her story about Beans as blackmailer stand up. And at the moment, only she knows that.''

Frank sipped his lukewarm tea. ''You really think Beans was going to blackmail her about the other thing, her lying about her age?''

''My best guess?'' Don paused. ''I doubt it. I'm sure that's what she thought, but I reckon that was just a case of, you know, don't judge others by your own standards.''

Their conversation was interrupted by a DC, who

handed Don a folded sheet of notepaper. Don unfolded the note, read it, and showed it to Frank.

"Right," he said. "Let's see if it's time to rejoin the ladies, shall we?"

"MY CLIENT HAS already admitted to killing Arthur Jones," said Kate Ferrold, once the tape was running again. "And she has fully and frankly described the circumstances which led to this tragic event. The killing was not in any way premeditated. My client deeply regrets the death of Mr. Jones. She will co-operate with you fully in all your inquiries into this matter, but she does not see any need whatsoever to alter the statement she has already given you."

So that's it, thought Frank. Don was right: given a decent barrister and a hormonal judge, she'd be out in five years. He looked sideways at the DI, and saw the slumped shoulders of deflated hope.

"They've found the body, by the way," Don said, as if to himself.

"Body?" said Dill. Her lawyer threw her a warning glance.

"The body on Plot 14," said Don. "Your father's wife."

"Right," said Dill. "Yes…yes, right, thank you."

Kate Ferrold looked from Dill to Don and back again. Something was wrong here, her look said, and she didn't know what it was. But she knew what to do about it. "If you have no further questions for my—"

"You didn't know, did you?" said Don, staring straight at Dill, ignoring her lawyer's squawks of protest and warning. "You didn't think there was a body there, did you?" He stood up, and paced the room.

Frank watched him with growing trepidation, remembering the terrifying interview with Mr. Perfect.

"I finally see it all," said Don, as Dill remained mute and pale. "You came back to England, just as you originally told us, for a fresh start. But why? Why did you need to? I bet when we start talking to the Canadian authorities, we'll find you pulled a stunt like the Natural Beauty one over there, too. Or something along similar lines. You're a con woman, Moira, aren't you? That's where your money comes from, to pay for your rented semi and your jobless lifestyle and your fancy lawyer."

"Inspector!" barked the fancy lawyer. "I must insist—"

"So when it went wrong in Canada you took advantage of your British passport to come here. To start again. Make another fortune. Why here, specifically, why Cowden, I don't know. Sentimental reasons, maybe. At any rate, it's all going fine until you realise that Beans knows who you are. And knows, at least to the nearest decade, when you were born. He knew your mother, didn't he? As well as your father. You, being the sort of person you are, think he's going to blackmail you or expose you, or maybe just open his big mouth about you. And so he has to die. And it's only then that you remember this crazy story your dad told you on his deathbed, out of his mind on painkillers, about burying a body on his old allotment. You never believed him, of course, and I daresay your mother told you, 'Oh take no notice, that's just the poor old soul's mind wandering.' But now that you need a fall-back story, against the day you might be arrested—"

"Inspector!" This time the lawyer would be heard. "My client has nothing more to say. She is distressed and fatigued and I insist that you end this interview immediately."

Don sank back into his chair. "Yeah, all right," was all he said. "Why not?"

"YOU FANCY A DRINK, Frank?" They were back in the corridor; Dill was back in her cell.

Frank heard the emptiness in Don's voice. "What, over the pub?"

"No—not the pub today. Wine bar. You want to split a bottle of red wine? Or three?"

No thanks, thought Frank. No thank you. Some things are above and beyond the call of duty. "I think I'll call it a day, actually, if it's all the same to you."

"Yeah," said Don. "Don't blame you. You get home to Debbie."

Oh God, thought Frank. Look at the poor bastard. "Well, we got her anyway," he said. "I mean, whatever the ins and outs—she didn't get away."

Don sighed, scratched his scalp. "It's not up to us, obviously; it'll be for the Crown Prosecution Service to decide. But I'll bet you anything they go with the body on Plot 14 as the motive. That other stuff, lying about her age for the cosmetics company—it's too complicated to sell to a jury. Even if we could prove it."

Frank couldn't think of anything comforting to say in reply to that, so he said goodbye instead, and walked off towards his locker, and home. *He'll be all right,* he told himself. *He's survived this long without*

*me, I don't need to feel guilty about abandoning him
tonight.*

"Frank?"

He turned: Lucy, waving a piece of fax roll at him.

"Been looking for you, Boy Detective," she said,
with a flirty smile. "Your Mr. Packham wanted the
prints done on that sheet of paper from Moira Mc-
Lennan's compost heap, yeah? Some photocopy of a
newspaper cutting."

"Oh, right, thanks, Lucy," said Frank, taking the
sheet, scanning it. "I'll see he gets it." That's right:
Don had asked for the prints to be worked up, and
Frank had said, *But obviously her prints'll be on it;
she admits handling it.* Frank hadn't got it: what was
the point? And Don had obviously forgotten all about
it.

According to Dill, Beans had shown her the cutting,
taunted her with it, causing her to lose her temper and
kill him. After which, she had taken it and hidden it
in her compost heap.

But now, reading the fax, Frank finally did get it.

Only one set of prints was found on the photocopy
sheet: that of Moira McLennan. Which meant it had
never been in Arthur Jones's possession. It was hers,
not her victim's. She had brought it to the allotments,
not him.

Which meant premeditation.

Lucy was still standing there, still smiling. Frank
smiled too.

"Got to run, Lucy! Got to catch up with Don Packham before he—before he leaves for the night. Only
I think I've got something here that might make even
him smile."

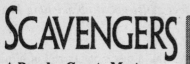

SCAVENGERS

A Posadas County Mystery

Steven F. Havill

A man's body is found in the
unforgiving New Mexico desert,
the beginning of a brutal murder
spree that has roots on both
sides of the border.

Retired sheriff Bill Gastner
offers unerring logic and
horse sense to new undersheriff
Estelle Reyes-Guzman in her
attempts to identify the "Juan" Doe.
When another body turns up in a
shallow grave and a suspicious fire
takes a third life, the terrible twist
finally offers the break Estelle has
been looking for, one that will lead
her back into a harsh, merciless
desert where death welcomes all.

"...there's solid pleasure to be derived
from Havill's consistently good writing,
colorful cast, and dead-on sense of place."
—*Kirkus Reviews*

Available February 2004 at your favorite retail outlet.

WSFH482

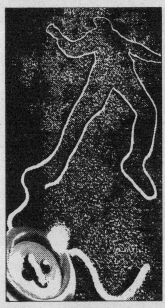

BUTTONS & FOES

A MANDY DYER MYSTERY

Dolores Johnson

Denver dry cleaner Mandy Dyer is shocked to learn that a favorite customer has died and left Mandy something—two trash bags packed with worthless old clothing. Full of questions, Mandy notices some antique buttons sewn onto the dresses and suspects the woman was trying to send her a message.

Convinced the button mystery is linked to her friend's sudden demise, Mandy starts nosing around the local button-collecting clubs...and stumbles onto another murder. And while removing bloodstains may be a cinch for an expert dry cleaner, Mandy hopes she won't have to try her luck against a cold-blooded killer.

"...entertaining, amusing amateur sleuth."
—Harriet Klausner

Available March 2004.

W✦RLDWIDE LIBRARY®

WDJ487

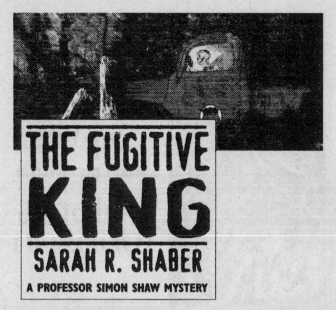

THE FUGITIVE KING

SARAH R. SHABER

A PROFESSOR SIMON SHAW MYSTERY

When the remains of a young woman who disappeared forty years ago are found in North Carolina, the man who went to prison for her murder wants history professor Simon Shaw to prove that he didn't kill her.

Putting small-town gossip, obliging relatives and old memories to good use, Shaw investigates. But what would drive a man to confess to a murder he didn't commit? A second murder disguised as an accident points Shaw in the right direction, leading him to a stunning discovery hidden deep in the hills, to a secret worth lying—and killing—for.

"An engaging mystery in a too-little-known series."
—*Booklist*

Available March 2004 at your favorite retail outlet.

WSRS485

COLD COMFORT

Scott Mackay

A Detective Barry Gilbert Mystery

When the stepdaughter of a prominent politician is found frozen with a bullet through her heart, overworked, underpaid homicide detective Barry Gilbert inherits the case.

The bizarre nature of the crime doesn't bode well for a quick and tidy solution. The victim's apartment was trashed and the intruder killed her parrot. She was never seen leaving her building on the security videotape. Add a large sum of stolen money and a dead sister and Gilbert is tackling a crime filled with dark secrets, dangerous relations and a killer convinced he can get away with murder.

"The twists and turns...recall the work of procedural master Hillary Waugh."
—*Ellery Queen Mystery Magazine*

Available March 2004.

 WORLDWIDE LIBRARY ®

WSM486

THE
MAINE
MULCH
MURDER

AN AMY CREIGHTON MYSTERY

A. CARMAN
CLARK

When 60-year-old Amy Creighton
finds the body of a young man in a
mulch pile, she is as stunned as the
rest of her small town. Amy is quickly
pulled into a mystery that threatens
to expose some dark secrets about
the inhabitants of her historic locale.

Amy and the local constable join
forces and discover that the victim
came to town looking for his birth
parents. But what fatal truths did he
learn? A second murder victim adds
a twisted thread of greed and money
to the mystery—and opens the door
to a shocking and tragic conclusion.

**"More than a traditional mystery,
this book offers an honestly written
look at two independent people who
get another chance."**
— *The Mystery Review*

*Available February 2004
at your favorite retail outlet.*

WORLDWIDE LIBRARY ®

WACC483